Hermann Hesse was born in Germany, at Calw, Württemberg, on 2 July 1877. He began his career as a bookseller and started to write and publish poetry at the age of twenty-one. Five years later he enjoyed his first major success with his novels on youth and educational problems: first *Peter Camenzind* (1904), then *The Prodigy* (1905), followed by *Gertrude* (1910), *Rosshalde* (1914), *Knulp* (1915) and *Demian* (1919). Later, when as a protest against German militarism in the First World War he settled permanently in Switzerland, he established himself as one of the greatest literary figures of the German-speaking world. Hesse's deep humanity and searching philosophy were further developed in such masterly novels as *Siddhartha* (1922), *Steppenwolf* (1927), and *Narziss and Goldmund* (1930), which together with his poems and a number of critical works won him a leading place among contemporary thinkers. In 1946 he won the Nobel Prize for Literature. Hermann Hesse died in 1962 shortly after his eighty-fifth birthday.

HERMANN HESSE

Klingsor's Last Summer

Translated from the German by
Richard and Clara Winston

TRIAD PALADIN
GRAFTON BOOKS

LONDON GLASGOW
TORONTO SYDNEY AUCKLAND

Triad/Paladin
Grafton Books
8 Grafton Street, London W1X 3LA

Published in Triad/Paladin Books 1989
Previously published by Triad/Panther 1985

Triad Paperbacks Ltd is an imprint of
Chatto, Bodley Head & Jonathan Cape Ltd and
Grafton Books, A Division of the Collins Publishing Group

First published in Great Britain by
Jonathan Cape Ltd 1971
Originally published in German under the title
Klingsors Letzter Sommer
Copyright S. Fischer Verlag, 1920
Translation © Farrar, Straus and Giroux, Inc. 1970

ISBN 0-586-08610-2

Printed and bound in Great Britain by
Collins, Glasgow

Set in Imprint

A Child's Heart

Chapter One

Sometimes we act, go in and out, do this and that, and everything is easy, casual, and unforced; seemingly it could all be done differently. And sometimes, other times, nothing could be done differently, nothing is unforced and easy, and every breath we take is controlled by some outside power and heavy with fate.

What we call the good deeds of our lives, the ones we find easy to tell about, are almost all of that first, 'easy' kind, and we easily forget them. Other acts, which we find hard to talk about, we never forget; they seem to be more ours than the others, and they cast long shadows over all the days of our lives.

Our father's house stood tall and bright on a sunlit street. You entered it through a high gate and at once found yourself embraced by coolness, dusk, and stony moist air. A high dark hall silently received you; the red sandstone squares of the flooring led at a slight incline to the stairs, which lay far at the rear, in semi-darkness. Many thousands of times I entered through that high gate, and never did I pay attention to gate and hallway, stone flooring and stairs. For these were always merely a passage into another world, 'our' world. The hall smelled of stone; it was dusky and high. At the rear of it, the stairs led up out of the dim coolness into light and bright cosiness. But the hall and the sombre duskiness always came first. There was something of Father about it, something of dignity and power, something of punishment and guilty conscience. A thousand times I passed through, laughing. But sometimes I stepped inside and at once felt crushed and reduced, afraid, and I hurried to the liberating stairs.

One day when I was eleven years old I came home from school. It was one of those days when fate lurks in the corners, when something can easily happen. On such days every failing and disturbance in our own souls seems to be reflected in our surroundings, distorting them. Uneasiness and anxiety grip our hearts, and we seek and find their presumed cause outside us. We see the world as ill-arranged and are met by obstacles everywhere.

That was how it was on that day. From early morning on, I was dogged by a sense of guilty conscience. Who knows what its source was – perhaps dreams of the night. For I had done nothing particularly bad. That morning my father's face had worn a suffering and reproachful expression. The breakfast milk had been lukewarm and insipid. Although I had not run into any trouble at school, everything had once more felt dreary, lifeless, and discouraging; everything had combined to form that already familiar feeling of helplessness and despair which tells us that time is endless, that eternally and forever we shall be small and powerless and remain under the rule of this stupid, stinking school, for years and years, and that this whole life is senseless and loathsome.

I had also been vexed by my best friend on that day. Lately I had struck up a friendship with Oskar Weber, the son of a locomotive engineer, without really knowing what drew me to him. He had recently boasted that his father earned seven marks a day, and I had answered at random that my father earned fourteen. He had let that impress him without argument, and that had been the beginning of the thing. Before the week was out I formed a league with Weber. We set up a joint savings account to be used later to buy a pistol. The pistol was displayed in a hardware shop's window, a massive weapon with two blued steel barrels. And Weber had calculated that we only had to save hard for a while and we would be able to buy it. Money was easy to come by; he was often given ten pfennig for errands, or picked up a tip here and there, and sometimes you found money on the street, or things worth money, like horseshoes, pieces of lead, and other things that could be easily sold. Moreover, he promptly contributed a ten-pfennig piece for our savings, and that convinced me and made our whole plan seem both feasible and hopeful.

As I entered the hall of our house that noon and in the cool, cellar-like air felt dark admonishments of a thousand bothersome and hateful things and systems wafting into my face, my thoughts were preoccupied with Oskar Weber. I felt that I did not love him, although I rather liked his good-natured face, which reminded me of a washerwoman's. What

attracted me to him was not himself but something else – I might say,
his class. It was something that he shared with almost all boys of his
type and origins: a kind of cheeky facility with life, a thick skin that protected him from danger and humiliation, a familiarity with the small,
practical affairs of life, with money, stores and workshops, with goods
and prices, with kitchens and laundries and things of that sort. Boys
like Weber, who seemed impervious to the blows dealt out in school,
who were kindred to and friendly with hired hands, draymen, and
factory girls, stood differently and more securely in the world than I
did. They knew how much their fathers earned in a day and undoubtedly knew many other things about which I was wholly inexperienced. They laughed at expressions and jokes that I did not understand.
Altogether, they could laugh in a way that was closed to me, in a filthy
and coarse but undeniably grownup and 'manly' way. It did not help
that I was smarter than they and knew more in school. It did not help
that I was better dressed, combed, and washed. On the contrary, these
very differences were to their credit. It seemed to me that boys like
Weber could enter without trouble into the 'world', as it appeared to
me in a nimbus of strangeness and glamour, while the 'world' was so
utterly closed to me that I would have to conquer each of its gates by a
wearisome, endless process of growing older, sitting in school, examina-
tions, and upbringing. It was only natural that such boys also found
horseshoes, money, and pieces of lead in the street, that they were paid
for errands, received all sorts of gifts in shops, and thrived in every
possible way.

I felt obscurely that my friendship with Weber and his savings was
nothing but a wild longing for that 'world'. There was nothing lovable
about Weber but his great secret, by virtue of which he stood closer to
adults than I did and lived in a more naked, less veiled, more robust
world than I did with my dreams and wishes. And I sensed beforehand
that he would disappoint me, that I would not be able to wrest from
him his secret and the magic key to life.

He had just left me and I knew he was now on his way home, thickset
and smug, whistling and cheerful, troubled by no longings, no forebodings. When he met the housemaids and factory girls and saw them
leading their mysterious, perhaps wonderful, perhaps criminal life,
it was no mystery to him, no vast secret, no danger; it was nothing wild
and exciting, but as natural, familiar, and homelike as water is to a
duck. That was how it was. And I, for my part, would always stand outside, alone and uncertain, full of intimations but without certainty.

Altogether, on that day life once again tasted hopelessly pallid. The day had some of the quality of a Monday, although it was a Saturday. It smelled of Monday, three times as long and three times as dreary as the other days. Life was damned and disgusting, horrid and full of falsehood. The grownups acted as if the world were perfect and as if they themselves were demigods, we children nothing but scum. These teachers . . . ! I felt striving and ambition within myself; I made sincere and passionate efforts to be good, whether in learning the Greek irregular verbs or in keeping my clothes clean. I struggled to achieve obedience to my parents or silent stoicism before all pain and humiliation. Again and again I rose up, ardent and devout, prepared to dedicate myself to God and to tread the ideal, pure, noble path towards the heights, to practice virtue, to suffer evil silently, to help others. And alas, again and again it remained only a beginning, an attempt, a brief fluttering flight! Again and again, after a few days, even after a few hours, something happened that should not have been allowed, something wretched, depressing, and shaming. Again and again, in the midst of the noblest and staunchest decisions and vows, I fell abruptly, inescapably, into sin and wickedness, into ordinary bad habits. Why was it this way? Why could I recognize so clearly the beauty and rightness of good intentions, could feel them so deeply within my heart, when all of life (including the adults) reeked everlastingly of ordinariness and everything was so arranged that shabbiness and vulgarity triumphed? How could it be that in the morning on my knees at my bedside, or at night before lighted candles, I could pledge myself to goodness and the light, could appeal to God and renounce all sin forever and ever – only to commit, perhaps but a few hours later, the most wretched betrayals of this same solemn oath and sincerest resolution, if only by chiming in with tempting laughter, or by lending an ear to a stupid schoolboy joke? Why was that so? Was it different for others? Had heroes, the Romans and Greeks, the knights, the first Christians – had all these others been different from myself, better, more perfect, without bad impulses, equipped with some organ that I lacked, which prevented them from forever falling back from heaven into everyday life, from the sublime into inadequacy and wretchedness? Was original sin unknown to heroes and saints? Was holiness and nobility possible only for a few rare, elect souls? But why, if I were not one of the elect, why was this impulse towards beauty and nobility innate in me? Why did I have this wild, painful longing for purity, goodness, and virtue? Was I being made mock of? Could it possibly be, in God's world, that a person, a boy, would simultaneously have all the sublime and all the evil impulses within himself and be forced to suffer and despair, to cut an unhappy and ridiculous figure, for the amusement of God as he looked on? Could that be so? Rather, wasn't – yes, wasn't the whole world a joke of the devil that ought to be spewed out? If that were so, then was not God a monster , insane, a stupid, horrible prankster? . . . And even as I had this thought, with a faint savour of voluptuous delight in rebellion, my fearful heart punished me for the blasphemy by pounding furiously!

How clearly I see, after thirty years, that stairwell with the tall opaque windows giving on the wall of the house next door and casting so little light, with the white-scoured pine steps and risers and the smooth wooden banister polished from my innumerable sliding descents. Distant as my childhood is, and incomprehensible and fabulous though it seems to me on the whole, I still sharply remember all the suffering and doubts I felt at the time, in the midst of happiness. All those reelings existed in the child's heart, where they have been ever since: doubt of my own worth, vacillation between self-esteem and discouragement, between idealistic contempt for the world and ordinary sensuality. And just as I did then, I later continued to regard these aspects of my nature sometimes as a miserable morbidity, sometimes as a distinction. At times I believed that God wished to lead me on this painful path to a special isolation and deepening of my nature, at other times I took it all as nothing but the signs of shabby weakness of character, of a neurosis such as thousands of people bear wearisomely through their lives.

If I were to reduce all my feelings and their painful conflicts to a single name, I can think of no other word but: dread. It was dread, dread and uncertainty, that I felt in all those hours of shattered childhood felicity: dread of punishment, dread of my own conscience, dread of stirrings in my soul which I considered forbidden and criminal.

At that hour I have been speaking of, this sense of dread once again struck me as I drew nearer to the glass door at the top of the stairs, where the light grew brighter and brighter. The feeling began with a tightness in my stomach that rose to my throat and there became a choking or gagging sensation. Along with this at such moments, and now also, I felt a painful sense of embarrassment, a distrust of all observers, an urge to be alone and to hide.

With this repulsive feeling, truly the feeling of a criminal, I entered the hall and then the living room. I sensed that the devil was afoot today, that something was going to happen. I sensed it as the barometer senses a change in the pressure of the air, with utterly helpless passivity. Ah, here it was again, the inexpressible horror. The demon was skulking through the house. Original sin gnawed at my heart. Vast and invisible, a ghost stood behind every wall, a father and judge.

As yet I knew nothing. It was all mere foreboding, a gnawing, antici-patory uneasiness. In such situations it was often best to fall ill, to throw up and go to bed. Then the dangerous time sometimes passed harm-lessly; Mother or Sister came in, I would be given tea and felt sur-rounded by loving solicitude. I could cry or sleep, and afterwards waken sound and cheerful in a wholly transformed, relaxed, and bright world.

My mother was not in the living room, and only the maid was in the kitchen. I decided to go up to Father's study at the top of a narrow flight of stairs. Although I was also afraid of him, it was sometimes good to turn to him whom I had to ask forgiveness for so many things. With Mother it was easier and simpler to find comfort; but Father's comfort was more valuable. It meant peace with the judging conscience, recon-ciliation and a new covenant with the good powers. After nasty scenes, interrogations, confessions, and punishments I had often emerged good and pure from Father's room, punished and reproved, to be sure, but full of fresh resolutions, strengthened by the pact with power against the evil enemy. I decided to visit Father and tell him that I was feeling ill.

And so I climbed the short flight of stairs that led to the study. These stairs, with their own special wallpaper smell and the dry sound of the light, hollow wooden treads, were infinitely more fraught with signi-ficance and fatefulness than even the entrance hall. Many important causes had led me up these steps; a hundred times I had dragged dread and a tormented conscience up them, or defiance and wild anger, and quite often I had returned down them with absolution and new security. In the dwelling below, mother and child were at home; the atmosphere was mild there. Up here power and spirit dwelt; up here were the court-house and temple and the 'realm of the father'.

Rather timidly, as always, I pressed down the old-fashioned latch and opened the door half way. The smell of the paternal study flowed towards me, the familiar smell of books and ink, attenuated by blue air from half-open windows, by white, clean curtains, a faint dash of cologne water, and an apple on the desk. But the room was empty.

With a sensation half of disappointment and half of relief, I entered. I checked my thumping footsteps, walked on tiptoe, as we often had to up here when Father was napping or had a headache. And as soon as I became aware of how quietly I was moving, my heart began to pound and I again felt, intensified, the anxious pressure in my stomach and my throat. I moved on, skulking and frightened, took a step and another step, and already I had ceased to be a harmless visitor and petitioner and had become an intruder. More than once I had secretly crept into Father's two rooms during his absence, had explored his secret realm, and twice I had filched something from it.

The memory of these thefts came at once and filled me, and I knew at once that disaster was upon me. Now something was going to happen, now I was doing something forbidden and evil. I had no thought of flight! Rather, I did think of it, thought fervently and longingly of running away, down the stairs and into my own room or into the garden – but I knew that I was not going to, that I could not. How I wished that my father might stir in the adjacent room and come in and break the terrible spell that held me in its grip. If only he would come! If only he could come, scolding for all I cared, but come before it was too late!

I coughed to announce my presence, and when there was no answer I called softly: 'Papa!' All remained still; the many books on the walls gave no answer. A pane of the casement window moved in the wind, casting a glint of sunlight on the floor. No one redeemed me, and inside myself I had no freedom to do anything but the demon's bidding. A feeling of criminality contracted my stomach and made my fingertips cold; my heart fluttered with dread. As yet I had no idea what I would do. I knew only that it would be something naughty.

Now I was at the desk. I picked up a book and read a title in English which I did not understand. I hated English – my father always spoke it with Mother when we children were not supposed to understand, and also when they were quarrelling. In a bowl lay all sorts of small objects, toothpicks, pen points, tacks. I took two of the pen points and pocketed them. God knows why; I did not need them, had no lack of pens. I did it only to obey the compulsion that was almost choking me, the compulsion to do something bad, to harm myself, to load myself with guilt. I leafed through my father's papers, saw a letter he had begun, read the words, 'We and the children are very well, thank God,' and the Latin letters of his handwriting looked at me like so many eyes.

Then I stole softly into the bedroom. There stood Father's iron army bed, his brown house slippers under it, a handkerchief on the night table. I inhaled the paternal air in the cool, bright room, and the image of my father rose plainly before my eyes, while reverence and rebellion contested in my overladen heart. For moments I hated him, remembering with spite and malice how he sometimes, on headache days, lay still and flat on his low cot, stretched out at great length, a wet towel on his forehead, sometimes sighing. Certainly I had an inkling that he too, for all his power, had no easy life; that he, of whom I stood in such awe, also experienced timidity and doubts of himself. In a moment my strange hatred evaporated and was followed by pity and sentiment. But in the meanwhile I had opened one of the drawers of his chest. There his linens lay in neat layers, and a bottle of cologne water, which he was fond of. I wanted to sniff it, but the bottle was still unopened and firmly capped; I put it back. Next to it I found a small round box of lozenges which had a liquorice taste. I popped a few of them into my mouth. A sense of disappointment overcame me, and at the same time I was glad not to have found and taken anything more.

Already renouncing and preparing to leave, I playfully pulled at one more drawer, my heart somewhat lightened, so that I could promise myself to replace the two stolen pen points. Perhaps a return to grace was possible. Perhaps all could be made good again and I would be saved. God's hand above me might be stronger than all temptation. . .

I peeped into the crack of the barely opened drawer. Oh, if only socks or shirts or old newspapers had been in it. But there was the temptation, and instantly the tension and the spell of fear returned; my hands trembled and my heart pounded madly. I was looking into a wicker basket, of Indian or some other exotic origin, and there I saw something surprising, alluring: a whole round of pale, sugar-coated dried figs!

I picked it up. It was wonderfully heavy. Then I took two or three figs, put one into my mouth, the others in my pocket. All my fear and excitement had in the end not been in vain. I could no longer leave here feeling redeemed and assuaged; so at least I did not want to leave empty-handed. I took another two or three figs from the ring, which was scarcely lightened, and then a few more, and when my pockets were filled and more than half the round had disappeared, I arranged the remaining figs more loosely on the somewhat sticky rope so that fewer seemed to be missing. Then, in sudden panic, I banged the drawer shut and ran away, through both rooms, down the small staircase and into my room, where I stood still, leaning against my little desk, my knees weak and my lungs gasping for breath.

Soon afterwards our dinner bell rang. With my head empty, filled with depression and disgust, I stuffed the figs into my bookshelf, hiding them behind books, and went to table. At the dining-room door I noticed that my hands were sticky. I washed them in the kitchen. In the dining room I found everyone already at table. I quickly said Good day, Father said grace, and I bent over my soup. I was not hungry; every spoonful was hard to swallow. And beside me sat my sisters, my parents opposite me, all of them bright and cheerful and honourable. I alone, the only criminal, sat wretchedly among them, alone and unworthy, fearing every friendly look, the taste of the figs still in my mouth. Had I closed the bedroom door upstairs? And the drawer?

Now the misery was upon me. I would have let my hand be chopped off if that could have restored my figs to the drawer. I decided to throw the figs away, to take them to school and give them away. If only I were rid of them, if only I never had to see them again!

'You're not looking well today,' my father said across the table. I stared at my plate, feeling his eyes on my face. Now he would see it. He saw everything, always. Why was he torturing me beforehand? He might as well lead me away right then and there and beat me to death for all I cared.

'Is something the matter with you?' I heard his voice again. I lied; I said I had a headache.

'You must lie down for a little after eating,' he said. 'How many more hours of school do you have this afternoon?'

'Only gym.'

'Well, gym will do you no harm. But eat something; force yourself a little. It will pass.'

I squinted across the table. My mother said nothing, but I knew that she was looking at me. I ate my soup, fought with the meat and vegetables, poured myself two glasses of water. Nothing more happened. I was left alone. When my father spoke the closing grace at the end of the meal, 'Lord, we thank thee, for thou art kindly and thy goodness lasteth eternally,' something severed me from the bright, holy, confident words and from all who sat at table with me. My folding my hands was a lie, my pious posture a blasphemy.

When I stood up, Mother brushed her hand over my hair and let her palm rest on my forehead for a moment to see whether it was hot. How bitter all that was!

In my room I stood before the bookshelf. The morning had not deceived me; all the signs had been correct. This had become a day of misfortune, the worst I had ever experienced; no human being could endure anything worse. If anything worse ever came upon a person, he would have to take his life. Poison was the best way, or hanging. It was better anyhow to be dead than alive. Everything was so wrong and ugly.

I stood there thinking these thoughts, and abstractedly reached out for one of the hidden figs and ate it, and then several more, without really knowing that I was doing it.

I noticed our savings bank, standing on the shelf beneath the books. It was a cigar box that I had nailed closed. With my penknife I had nicked out a crude slit in the lid for the coins. The slit was crudely cut; splinters of wood bristled from it. Even that I could not do properly. I had playmates who could do that sort of thing laboriously and patiently and properly, so that it looked like a cabinetmaker's work. But I always botched such things; I was in a hurry and never finished anything neatly. I was like that with my woodworking, like that with my hand-writing and my drawing, like that with my butterfly collection and everything. I was hopeless. And now I stood here and had stolen again, worse than ever before. I still had the pen points in my pocket. What for? Why had I taken them – been compelled to take them? Why did I have to do something I did not want to do at all?

A single coin rattled in the cigar box, Oskar Weber's ten-pfennig piece. Since then nothing had been added. This savings-bank business was another one of my typical undertakings! Everything came to noth-ing, everything went wrong; whatever I began bogged down at the start. The devil take this idiotic savings bank! I wanted to have nothing more to do with it.

This period between lunch and the afternoon session of school was always wretched and hard to get through on days like today. On good days, on peaceful, sensible, pleasant days, these two hours were lovely and longed-for. Then I would either read an Indian book in my room or run back to the schoolyard immediately after eating. There I would always find a few enterprising classmates and we would play, shouting and running and getting hot, until the ringing of the bell called us back to a completely forgotten 'reality'. But on days like today I did not want to play with anyone, and how could I silence the devil in my heart? I saw what was coming – not yet, not today, but soon, perhaps the next time. One day my fate would descend fully upon me. All that was lack-ing was a trifle, a mere trifle more of dread and suffering and perplexity, and then it would overflow, then all would end in horror. One day, on just such a day as today, I would be wholly drowned in evil; in defiance and rage and because of the senseless unbearableness of this life I would do something ghastly and decisive, something ghastly but liberating which would forever make an end of the dread and torment. I did not know what it would be; but fantasies and preliminary obsessions about it

had more than once run confusingly through my head, notions of crimes
with which I would take revenge upon the world and at the same time
abandon and destroy myself. Sometimes I thought I would set fire to
our house. I saw monstrous flames beating their wings into the night,
consuming houses and streets; the whole city would flare gigantically
against the black sky. Or at other times the crime was revenge against
my father, murder, a cruel killing. But I would then behave like that
criminal, that one real criminal, whom I had once seen being led
through the streets of our town. It was a burglar who had been caught
and was being led to court, handcuffed, a stiff bowler askew on his head,
a policeman in front of him and behind him. This man who was being
driven through the streets and through a huge crowd who shouted a
thousand curses, nasty jokes, and malignant wishes at him, this man in
no way resembled those timorous wretches I sometimes saw being ac-
companied across the street by a patrolman. Most of them were only
poor journeymen who had been caught begging. But this man was no
journeyman and did not look foolish, timid, and weepy, nor was he
taking refuge in a sheepish stupid grin, such as I had also seen. This
man was a real criminal and wore his somewhat crushed hat boldly on a
defiant and unbowed head. He was pale and smiling with quiet contempt; alongside such a man the populace reviling him became a rabble.
At the time I myself had shouted with the rest, 'They've caught him,
he ought to be hanged!' But then I saw his upright, proud posture, the
way he held his fettered hands in front of him, and the way he wore that
bowler hat like a fantastic crown on his head, and the way he smiled –
and I fell silent. But I too would smile like this criminal and hold my
head stiffly when they led me into court and to the scaffold and when all
the people around me crowded forward and shouted insults – I would
say neither yes nor no but would simply hold my tongue and despise
them.

And when I had been executed and was dead and came before the
eternal Judge in heaven, I would by no means bow down and submit.
Oh no, not though all the choirs of angels were gathered around him
and he radiated pure holiness and dignity. Let him damn me, let him
have me boiled in pitch! I would not apologize and not humble myself,
would not beg his forgiveness, would not repent! If he asked me: 'Did
you do such and such?' I would cry out, 'Yes, I did it, and more, and
I was right to have done it and if I can I will do it again and again. I
killed, I set fire to houses, because I enjoyed it and because I wanted
to mock and anger you. Because I hate you and I spit at your feet, God.

You have plagued me and hurt me, you have made laws nobody can keep, you have set grownups to make life a hell for us boys.'

Whenever I was able to imagine this scene with sufficient vividness, so that I felt I would really act and speak along these lines, I felt for moments gloomily good. But then came doubts. Would I not weaken, would I not quail, would I not give in after all? Or if I carried through as I was determined to do – would not God find a way out, some superior deception such as the grownups and the powerful always contrived, producing one more trump card at the last moment, shaming me after all, not taking me seriously, humiliating me under the damnable mask of kindliness? Ah yes, of course it would end like that.

My fantasies eddied back and forth, let me win one time, let God win another time, raised me up to a dauntless criminal and dragged me down again to a child and a weakling.

I stood at the window looking down at the small back yard of the house next door, where poles for scaffolding were leaning against the wall and a few beds of vegetables were sprouting green in a tiny garden. Suddenly, in the afternoon stillness, I heard the clang of bells intruding firmly and sombrely upon my visions: one clear, stern stroke for the hour, and then another. It was two o'clock, and I started out of my anxious daydreams and back to reality. Now our gym hour was beginning, and even if I had rushed off to the gymnasium on magic wings I would still have been late. More bad luck! Day after tomorrow I would be called up, scolded, punished. I might as well not go at all; there was no way to rectify things now. Perhaps if I had a very good, very subtle and believable excuse – but at the moment none occurred to me, brilliantly though our teachers had educated me in lying. Right now I was incapable of lying, inventing, constructing a story. It was better to stay away from school entirely. What did it matter if a small sin were added to the great one!

But the striking of the hour had roused me and numbed my fantasies. I felt suddenly very weak. My room glared at me with intense reality; desk, pictures, bed, books, were all charged with austere concreteness, all a summons from the world in which I had to live and which today had once more shown itself hostile and dangerous. Hadn't it? Had I not missed my gym class? And had I not stolen, wretchedly stolen, and weren't those damnable figs lying on the bookshelf, those I had not already devoured, that is? What did I care now about the criminal, God, and the Last Judgement! That would all come along in its own good time – but now, right at the moment, it was far away and was silly nonsense, nothing more. I had stolen and any moment the crime might be discovered. Perhaps it already had been, perhaps my father upstairs had already opened that drawer and was confronting my crime, offended and angered, considering the best way to bring me to trial. He might even be on his way down to my room already, and if I did not flee immediately, in another minute I would have his grave, bespectacled face before me. For of course he knew at once that I was the thief. There were no criminals in our house aside from me; my sisters never did anything bad. God knows why. But then why did my father have to keep such fig rings hidden in his chest of drawers?

I had already left my room and made off through the back door and the garden. The meadows and gardens lay in bright sunlight. Sulphur butterflies flew across the path. Everything looked threatening now, far worse than this morning. Oh, how well I knew this feeling, and yet I thought I had never felt it so painfully before. It was as if everything were looking at me with such matter-of-factness and such untroubled conscience, the town and the church tower, the fields and the path, the flowering grass and the butterflies, and as if everything pretty and pleasurable, everything that usually gave me delight, were now alien and under an evil spell. I was familiar with that, I knew the savour of it, when I ran along through the familiar neighbourhood with pangs of conscience. Now the rarest butterfly could flutter across the meadow and alight at my feet – it was nothing, gave no pleasure, did not tempt me, did not comfort me. Now the loveliest cherry tree could offer me its fullest branch – it had no value, there was no joy in it. Now there was nothing to do but flee, from Father, from punishment, from myself, from my conscience, to flee on and on until, inexorably and inescapably, everything that had to come would come anyhow.

I trotted along restlessly, I trudged uphill towards the woods and down from Oak Hill to the mill, across the footbridge and uphill again on the other side, and on through the woods. Here we had had our last Indian camp. Here, last year, when Father was away travelling, our mother had celebrated Easter with us children, hiding the eggs for us in the shrubbery and the moss. During the summer holidays I had once built a castle here with my cousins; it was still partly standing. Everywhere were vestiges of former times, everywhere mirrors out of which a child looked at me who was different from the child I was today. Had I been all those others? So gay, so contented, so grateful, so comradely, so affectionate towards Mother, so untouched by anxiety, so incomprehensibly happy? Had that been me? And how could I have become what I now was, so utterly different, so wicked, so full of dread, so distraught? Everything was the same as always, the woods and the river, the fern and the flowers, the castle and the anthill, and yet everything was poisoned, shattered. Was there no way back to happiness and innocence? Would what had been never be again? Would I ever again laugh like that, play with my sisters like that, hunt for Easter eggs like that?

I ran and ran, my forehead sweaty, and behind me my guilt ran and with it, huge and fearsome, ran the shadow of my father in hot pursuit.

Lanes ran past me; the margins of the woods dropped away. I came to a halt on top of a hill, cut away from the path, threw myself into the grass, my heart pounding; that might be from running uphill, might stop if I rested. Below me I saw the town and the river, saw the gym where the class was now over and the boys were dashing off in all directions. I saw the long roof of our house. There was my father's bedroom and the drawer from which the figs were missing. There was my small room. There, when I returned, judgement would strike me. But suppose I did not return?

I knew I would. I always went back, every time. That was how it always ended. It was impossible to get away, impossible to flee to Africa or Berlin. I was small, had no money, and nobody would help me. Oh yes, if all children would unite and help one another! They were many; there were more children than parents. But not all children were thieves and criminals. Few were like me. Perhaps I was the only one. But no, I knew that such cases as mine were commoner than that – an uncle of mine had also stolen as a child and had done many bad things which I knew about from eavesdropping on my parents' conversation. That was how I learned everything worth knowing, secretly, by overhearing. But none of that helped me in the least, and even if that same uncle were here now, he would not help me. He had long since grown up; he was a pastor and would side with the grownups and leave me to my fate. They were all like that. Towards us children they were all somehow liars and swindlers; they played a part, pretended to be different from what they were. Perhaps not Mother, or she less than others.

But suppose I didn't go back home? After all, something could happen to me; I could break my neck or drown or fall under the train. Then everything would be different. Then they would carry me home and everyone would be quiet and frightened and crying;

they would all feel sorry for me and nothing would ever be said about the figs.

I knew quite well that it was possible for a person to take his own life. I also thought that some day I would probably do it, later, when everything turned out altogether bad. It would have been good to be sick, but not just with a cough. Really deathly ill, the way I had been the time I had scarlet fever.

Meanwhile it was long past gym class, and also long past the time I was expected home for coffee. Perhaps they were calling and looking for me now, in my room, in the garden and yard, in the basement. But if Father had already discovered the theft, there would be no more searching, for then he would know why I was gone.

I could not go on just lying here. Fate was not forgetting me; it was right at my heels. I began running again. I passed a bench along one of the paths. Another memory was attached to that, a memory that had once been lovely and now burned like fire. My father had given me a penknife. We had gone walking together, in good spirits and at peace, and he had sat down on this bench while I went into the bushes to cut myself a long hazel switch. And then, in my excitement, I broke the blade of the new knife close to the haft and came back to him horrified. At first I wanted to conceal it, but he promptly asked me about the knife. I was terribly unhappy, because of the knife and because I expected a scolding. But then my father had only smiled, touched my shoulder lightly, and said: 'What a pity, poor boy.' How I had loved him then; how I had inwardly begged his forgiveness for so many things. And now, thinking of my father's expression at that time, of his voice and his sympathy – what a monster I was for having so often saddened and lied to a father like that, and today stolen from him!

When I reached the town again, near the upper bridge and far from our house, twilight was already falling. Lights were already lit in the shop windows. A boy came running out of a shop, stopped abruptly, and called my name. It was Oskar Weber. The last person I wanted to see. Still, I learned from him that the teacher had not noticed my absence from gym class. But where had I been?

'Oh, nowhere,' I said. 'I wasn't feeling well.'

I was taciturn and unfriendly, and after a while, which seemed to me outrageously long, he realized that I wanted to be rid of him. Then he turned nasty.

'Let me alone,' I said coldly. 'I can go home by myself.'

'Really?' he snapped. 'I can just as well walk by myself as you, dumbbell! I'm not your poodle, if you want to know. But first what about our savings bank? I put a tenner in it and you haven't put in anything.'

'You can have your tenner back today if you're worried about it. I wish I never had to see you again. Do you think I'd take anything from you!'

'You were glad enough to take it not so long ago,' he sneered, though he still left open a crack for reconciliation.

But I was hot and angry. All my accumulated fear and helplessness erupted in sheer rage. Weber had nothing to complain about! I was in the right; I had a clear conscience towards him. And I needed someone to make me feel proud and in the right by contrast. All the chaos and bleakness inside me poured furiously into this channel. I did what I ordinarily was careful not to: I put on the gentleman's son, indicated that it was no loss to me to give up friendship with a street urchin. I told him there would be no more of his eating berries in our garden and playing with my toys. I felt myself coming to life again in red-hot fury. I had an enemy, one who was to blame, one I could come to grips with. All my vital impulses gathered together into this releasing, welcome, liberating fury, into fierce delight in hating the foe who this time was not within myself, who stood facing me, staring at me with eyes at first alarmed, then angry, whose voice I heard, whose recriminations I despised, whose abusive language I could top.

Side by side, in a swelling altercation, we walked down the darkening street. Here and there someone glanced out of a door at us. And all the rage and contempt I felt towards myself poured out upon the unfortunate Weber. When he began to threaten that he would tell on me to the gym teacher, I felt rapturous. He was putting himself in the wrong, showing meanness, strengthening me.

When we began fighting in the street, a few people stood still and watched us. We hit each other in stomach and face and kicked each other. For those few moments I had forgotten everything. I was in the right, was not a criminal; the thrill of combat seized me, and although Weber was the stronger, I was more agile, smarter, faster, and more furious. We grew hot and swung fiercely. When he desperately grabbed and tore my shirt collar, I felt with ecstasy the stream of cold air pouring over my burning skin.

And while we punched, kicked, tore, wrestled, and choked, we did not for a moment stop berating, insulting, and annihilating each other in words, words that grew steadily hotter, more foolish and malicious, more inventive and fantastic. And I was his superior in that, too; I was more malicious and inventive. If he said *louse*, I said *rat*. If he said *bastard*, I shouted *devil*. Both of us were bleeding without feeling a thing, and at the same time our curses and abuse mounted; we threatened each other with the gallows, wished we had knives to drive in each other's ribs and twist; each defiled the other's name, descent, and father.

That was the first and only time I fought such a fight to the end in the full fever of battle, with all the blows, all the cruelties, all the vituperation. I had often watched fights and listened with shuddering pleasure to the vulgar swearwords. Now I myself was shouting them as if I had been accustomed to them from the time I was small and had often practised using them. Tears ran from my eyes and blood over my mouth. But the world was glorious; it had meaning; it was good to live, good to hit out, good to bleed and make another bleed.

In memory I could never afterwards recall how this fight ended. At some point it was over; at some point I stood alone in the quiet darkness, recognized street corners and houses, was close to our own house. Slowly, the intoxication subsided; slowly the thunder and roar of wings ceased, and reality penetrated bit by bit to my senses, first of all to my eyes. There was the fountain. The bridge. Blood on my hand, torn clothes, stockings that had slipped down, pain in my knee, pain in my eye, cap gone – everything came to me gradually, became reality, registered. Suddenly I was exhausted. I felt my legs and arms trembling, groped for the wall of a building.

And there was our house. Thank God! All I knew in this world now was that there was refuge, peace, light, shelter. With a sigh of relief I pushed back the high gate.

Then, with the smell of stone and damp coolness, recollection suddenly poured over me, multiplied a hundredfold. Oh God! That was the smell of sternness, of law, of responsibility. Of Father and God. I had stolen. I was not a wounded hero returning home from the fray. I was not a poor child finding his way home to be bedded down by his mother with warmth and sympathy. I was a thief, a criminal. Up those stairs was no refuge, bed, and sleep for me, no food and tender care, no comfort and forgetfulness. What awaited me was guilt and judgement.

That evening, in the dusky hallway and stairwell, whose many steps I climbed with an effort, I think I breathed in for the first time in my life the cold of empty space, solitude, fate. I saw no way out, I had no plans, not even fear, nothing but that cold, harsh feeling: 'It must be so.' Clinging to the banister, I drew myself up the stairs. At the glass door I felt tempted to sit down on the step for one moment, to catch my breath. I did not do it; there was no point. I had to go in. As I opened the door, it suddenly occurred to me to wonder how late it was.

I entered the dining room. There they sat around the table and had just finished eating; a plate of apples was still on the table. It was nearly eight o'clock. I had never come home so late without permission, never been absent for supper.

'Thank God, here you are!' my mother exclaimed. I saw that she had been anxious about me. She ran towards me, then stopped in alarm when she saw my face and my dirtied, torn clothing. I said nothing and looked at no one, but I distinctly felt Father and Mother communicating with one another by looks. My father controlled himself; but although he said nothing I felt how angry he was. Mother took care of me. My face and hands were washed, bandages plastered on my cuts; then I was given supper. Sympathy and solicitude surrounded me. I sat quietly, deeply ashamed, feeling the warmth and enjoying it with a guilty conscience. Then I was sent to bed. I shook hands with Father without looking at him.

After I was in bed, Mother came in to me once more. She took my clothes from the chair and put others there for me, since tomorrow was Sunday. Then she began cautiously asking questions, and I had to tell her about my fight. She thought it bad but did not scold and seemed a little astonished that I was so depressed and timid about it. Then she left.

Now, I thought, she is convinced that everything is all right. I had quarrelled and fought and been bloodied, but by tomorrow that would all be forgotten. She did not know about the other thing, the thing that mattered. She had been disturbed, but affectionate and unconstrained. This meant that Father, too, probably knew nothing yet.

And now a terrible sense of disappointment overcame me. I realized that from the moment I had entered the house I had been filled with one intense, consuming desire. I had thought, wished, longed for nothing but that the thunderstorm would crash down upon me at once, that the judgement would descend, that the terror would become a reality and my frightful fear of it cease. I was prepared for anything, could have withstood anything. I wanted to be punished, beaten, locked up. I wanted Father to make me go hungry. I wanted him to curse and reject me. If only the dread and the suspense would end!

Instead, here I lay, had enjoyed love and care, was being gently

spared and not called to account for my sin, and had to go on waiting
and fearing still longer. They had forgiven me my torn clothes, my long
absence, missing my supper, because I was tired and bleeding and they
felt sorry for me, but above all because they had no inkling of the other
thing, because they knew only of my naughtiness and nothing of my
depravity. It would go doubly hard for me when it came to light. Perhaps, as they had once threatened in the past, they would send me to a
reformatory where I would have only stale, hard bread to eat and in all
the time not taken up by lessons would have to saw wood and clean
shoes, and where there were dormitories with monitors who would
beat me with a cane and wake me at four o'clock in the morning with
cold water. Or else would they turn me over to the police?

But at any rate, no matter what happened, a waiting period was facing
me again. I would have to suffer the dread for still longer, carry my
secret with me still longer, tremble at every look and footstep in the
house, and be unable to look anyone in the eye.

Or was it possible after all that my theft would not even be noticed?
That everything would remain as it was? That I had inflicted all this
anxiety and torment on myself for nothing. Oh, if that were to happen,
if that inexpressible wonder were possible, then I would begin a wholly
new life, would thank God and show myself worthy of such goodness
by living with utter purity and stainlessness from this moment on!
What I had tried so often before and always failed at would now be
possible; now my resolution and my will were strong enough, now after
this misery, this hell of torment. My whole being seized upon this wish-
ful thought and clung to it. Comfort rained down from heaven; a blue
and sunny future opened up before me. In the midst of these fantasies
I finally fell asleep and slept untroubled all through the good night.

Next morning was Sunday, and while still lying in bed I felt, like the
taste of a fruit, the peculiar, curiously mixed, but on the whole so precious Sunday feeling I had known ever since I began going to school.
Sunday morning was a good thing: sleeping late, no school, prospect of
a good dinner, no smell of teachers and ink, plenty of time to myself.
That was the main thing. Other, alien, less pleasant notes sounded also,
but they were weaker: churchgoing or Sunday school, family walk,
having to be careful of my fine clothes. That somewhat spoiled the
pure, good, precious taste and smell of Sunday – just as two desserts
eaten at the same time, say a pudding and a sauce that went with it, did
not quite fit together, or as sometimes candy or cookies bought in small
shops had a faint, annoying overtone of cheese or kerosene. You ate

them and they were good, but they were not perfect and radiant; there was something about them you had to overlook. Sunday was usually something like that, especially when I had to go to church or Sunday school, which fortunately was not always the case. If I did, the free day acquired an added taste of duty and boredom. And although walks with the whole family could often be very fine, usually something happened. There was a quarrel with my sisters, or I walked too fast or too slow, or I smeared resin on my clothes. Most of the time there was a catch to it.

All right, I could put up with that. I felt good. A vast amount of time had passed since yesterday. I had not forgotten my crime; I remembered it first thing in the morning; but now it was so long ago that the terrors had receded far away and become unreal. Yesterday I had atoned for my guilt, even though it was only by the pangs of conscience. I had suffered through a wretched, horrible day. Now I was once more inclined to trustfulness and innocence and no longer worried very much. The agony was not entirely dissipated; a note of threat and uneasiness still sounded inside my head, but it was much like the minor duties and bothers that marred the loveliness of Sunday.

At breakfast we were all cheerful. I was given the choice between church and Sunday school. As always, I preferred church. There at least I was let alone and my thoughts could wander. Moreover, the high, solemn chamber with its coloured windows often seemed beautiful and uplifting, and when I squinted my eyes and peered down the long, dusty nave to the organ I often saw wonderful pictures. The organ pipes towering out of the gloom frequently seemed like a radiant city of a hundred towers. Moreover, when attendance was sparse I had often managed to lose myself in a book of stories for the entire hour.

On this day I did not take a book along. Nor did it even occur to me to try some evasion as I had done in the past. That much was left of last night; I remembered my vows to be good and reconciled to God, my parents, and the world. Even my anger against Oskar Weber had entirely dissipated. If he had turned up, I would have received him in the friendliest spirit.

The service began. I sang the choral verses with the others; the hymn was 'Shepherd of thy sheep,' which we had learned by heart in school. Once again I noticed how the verses of a song seemed so entirely different in singing, especially when sung in the slow, limping fashion of church, from the way it was in reading or reciting from memory. In reading, the verses were a whole, they had meaning and consisted of phrases. In singing they consisted only of words, there were no phrases at all, no meaning emerged, but on the other hand the single, long-drawn-out words had a curiously strong, independent life of their own. Frequently mere syllables, meaningless in themselves, took forms of their own and soared off by themselves. For example, as we sang the lines, 'Shepherd of thy sheep who knowest naught of sleep, them that stumble darkly, thou wilt guide and keep,' they seemed without co-herence and meaning. I did not think of a shepherd or of sheep; I thought of nothing at all. Yet that was by no means boring. Single words, especially 'sle-eep', became so strangely full and lovely, rocked me so softly, and the 'stum-ble' sounded so mysterious and weighty, reminded me of 'stomach' and of dark, strongly emotional, half-under-stood things that I had inside my body. And along with all that, the music of the organ.

And then came the pastor and the sermon, which was always so in-comprehensibly long, and the strange state of listening in which for a long time I heard only the sound of the speaking voice floating in the air like a bell, then took in single words sharply and distinctly, along with their meaning, and tried to follow what was being said as long as I could. If only I had been permitted to sit in the choir instead of among all the men in the gallery. In the choir, where I had sat at church concerts, you sank deeply into heavy, isolated chairs, each of them a small, firm building, and overhead you had a strangely attractive, complex, net-like vault, and high up on the wall the Sermon on the Mount was painted in soft colours, and the blue and red garment of the Saviour against the pale blue sky was so delicate and such a pleasure to look at.

Sometimes the wood of the pew creaked. I disliked it intensely be-cause it was coated with a dreary yellow varnish which you always stuck to slightly. Sometimes a fly buzzed off into one of the windows, which had blue and red flowers and green stars painted at their tops, where they curved into a pointed arch. And then the sermon was suddenly over and I leaned forward to see the pastor disappearing into his narrow, dark tube of a stairway. Everyone sang again, with relief and very loudly, and then people stood up and poured out of the church. I tossed the coin I had been given into the collection plate, whose tinny sound went so ill with all the solemnity, and let the stream of people carry me to the doors and out into the open.

Now came the finest part of Sunday: the two hours between church and Sunday dinner. I had done my duty, and now after sitting so long

I was eager for movement, for games or walks, or for a book. At any rate, I was completely free until dinner, when there usually was something good to eat. Contentedly, I sauntered home, filled with amiable thoughts and purposes. The world was all right; it was livable. Peacefully, I trotted through the hallway and up the stairs.

The sun was shining in my room. I looked to my box of caterpillars, which I had neglected yesterday, found a few new cocoons, watered the plants.

Then the door opened.

I paid no attention at first. After a minute the silence began to seem strange. I turned around. There stood my father. He was pale and looked tormented. My welcome stuck in my throat. I saw that he knew. He had come. The trial was beginning. Nothing had turned out well, nothing was atoned for, nothing forgotten. The sun paled and the Sunday morning collapsed.

Thunderstruck, I stared at Father. I hated him. Why had he not come yesterday? Now I was not girded for this, had no resources, not even repentance and a sense of guilt. And why did he have to keep figs upstairs in his chest of drawers?

He went over to my bookcase, reached behind the books, and took out several figs. There were few left. As he did so, he looked at me with mute inquiry. I could not say anything. Anguish and defiance choked me.

'What's the matter?' I finally brought out.

'Where did you get these figs?' he asked me in that low, controlled voice I so bitterly hated.

I began talking at once. Lying. I said I had bought the figs at a confectioner's, that there had been a whole ring of them. Where did the money come from? From a savings box I had together with a friend. We'd pooled the small coins we were given every so often. Incidentally – here was the box. I produced the box with the slit. Now there was only a ten-pfennig piece left in it because we had bought the figs yesterday.

My father listened with a quiet, composed expression. Not for a moment did I believe he felt as calm as he looked.

'How much did the figs cost?' he asked in that soft voice.

'One mark sixty.'

'And where did you buy them?'

'At the confectioner's.'

'Which one?'

'Haager's.'

There was a pause. I was still holding the money box in my freezing fingers. My whole body was cold and shivering.

And now he asked, with a note of menace in his voice: 'Is that true?'

Again I talked rapidly. Yes, of course it was true, and my friend Weber had gone into the store, I had only tagged along with him. The money was mainly Weber's, only a little of it came from me.

'Take your cap,' my father said. 'We'll go over to Haager's together. He'll certainly remember selling you the figs.'

I tried to smile. Now the cold had penetrated as far as my heart and stomach. I led the way, picking up my blue cap in the hall. Father opened the glass door. He too had taken his hat.

'Just a moment,' I said. 'I have to go.'

He nodded. I went to the bathroom, locked the door, and was alone, safe for another moment. If only I could die now!

I stayed a minute, stayed two. It was no use. You didn't die. You had to face everything. I unlocked the door and we descended the stairs together.

As we were going out the front door, a happy thought struck me. I said quickly: 'But today is Sunday and Haager's isn't open.'

That hope lasted just two seconds. My father said calmly: 'Then we'll go to his house. Come.'

We walked. I straightened my cap, thrust one hand into my pocket, and tried to walk along beside him as though nothing in particular were happening. Although I knew that everybody could see I was a criminal who had just been caught, I tried by a thousand devices to conceal the fact. I struggled to breathe easily and innocently. Nobody needed to see how my whole chest was constricted. I tried to put on a candid expression, to pretend naturalness and security. I pulled up one of my stockings, though it did not need pulling, and smiled, knowing that this smile looked frightfully stupid and forced. The devil was inside me, in my throat and innards, and he was choking me.

We passed the restaurant, passed the blacksmith, passed the hansom-cab stand, passed the railroad bridge. This was where I had fought with Weber last night. Didn't the cut above my eye still hurt? Oh God! Oh God!

Docilely, I walked on, keeping my composure by terrible efforts. We started down Main Street. How amiable and harmless this street had seemed only yesterday. Must not think. On, on!

We were very close to Haager's house. During those few minutes I had several hundred times lived through in advance the scene that awaited me. Now we were there. Now it was coming.

But it was impossible to endure. I stood still.

'Well? What's the matter?' Father asked.

'I'm not going in,' I muttered.

He looked down at me. He had known from the start, of course. Why had he pretended all this and gone to so much trouble. There was no point to it.

'Then you didn't buy the figs at Haager's?' he asked.

I shook my head.

'I see,' he said with seeming calm. 'Then we might as well go back home.'

He behaved decently. He spared me on the street, in front of people. There were many people out walking; someone greeted my father every minute. What play-acting! What stupid, senseless torment! I could not be grateful to him for sparing me.

He knew everything, of course! And he let me dance, let me perform my useless capers the way you let a captive mouse dance in its wire trap before you drown it. If only he had hit me over the head with his cane right at the start, without asking me any questions at all! I would have preferred that to the calm and righteousness with which he caught me in my idiotic net of lies and slowly strangled me. Maybe it was better to have a coarse father than such a refined and just one. When the kind of father I read about in stories gave his children a terrible beating in rage or drunkenness, then the father was in the wrong, and although the blows hurt, the child could shrug his shoulders inwardly and despise him. With my father, that wouldn't do. He was too refined, too good, never in the wrong. He always made me feel small and wretched.

With clenched teeth I preceded him into the house and returned to my room. He was still quiet and cool, or rather pretending to be so, for in reality he was very angry, as I clearly felt. Now he began to talk in his usual way.

'I would like to know what the purpose of this farce is? Can't you tell me that? I knew at once that your whole pretty story was a lie. So why were you trying to make a fool of me? You don't seriously think me so stupid as to believe you?'

I continued to clench my teeth. I swallowed. If only he would stop. As if I myself had any idea why I had told him the story! As if I myself had any idea why I could not confess my crime and ask for forgiveness. As if I even had any idea why I had stolen those wretched figs. Had I wanted to? Had I done it on reflection and with reasons, knowing what I was doing? Wasn't I sorry I had done it? Wasn't I suffering because of it more than he?

He waited, his face nervous, tense with the effort of patience. For just a moment, in my unconscious, I fully understood the situation, but I could not have put it into words as I can today. It was this: I had stolen because I had gone into Father's room in need of comfort and because to my disappointment I had found it empty. I had not wanted to steal. When I found Father not there I had only wanted to spy, to poke among his things, to penetrate his secrets, to find out something about him. That was it. Then the figs lay there and I stole them. And I immediately regretted the act and all day yesterday I had suffered torment and despair, had wanted to die, had condemned myself, had conceived new, good resolutions. But today – today everything was different. I had tasted the repentance and all the rest to the full; I was less emotional now and felt inexplicable but enormous resistances towards my father and towards everything he expected and demanded of me.

If I had been able to tell him that, he would have understood me. But even children, though they are far ahead of adults in cleverness, are perplexed and alone when they confront fate.

Stiff with defiance and determined anguish, I kept silent, let him talk, and watched with pain and a strange gloating delight the way everything went wrong and turned worse and worse, how he suffered and was disappointed, how he appealed in vain to all my better instincts.

When he asked, 'Did you steal the figs?' I could only nod. I could not bring myself to do more than nod feebly when he wanted to know whether I was sorry. How could this big, intelligent man ask such foolish questions! As if I would not have been sorry! As if he could not see how the whole affair hurt me, how it twisted my heart. As if at this point I could have taken any pleasure in my act and in those wretched figs!

Perhaps for the first time in my life I felt, almost to the verge of understanding and consciousness, how utterly two well-intentioned human beings can torment each other, and how in such a case all talk, all attempts at wisdom, all reason merely adds another dose of poison, creates new tortures, new wounds, new errors. How was that possible? But it was possible, it was happening. It was absurd, it was crazy, it was ridiculous and desperate – but it was so.

Enough of this story. It ended with my being locked up in the attic all Sunday afternoon. This harsh punishment lost a part of its terrors for reasons that were my secret. For in that dark, unused attic there was a box, covered with dust, half full of old books, some of which were by no means intended for children. I made light for reading by pushing aside one of the roof tiles.

Shortly before I went to bed that sad Sunday night my father cajoled me into talking with him briefly, and that made peace between us. When I lay in bed I had the certainty that he had completely forgiven me – more completely than I had forgiven him.

Klein and Wagner

Chapter One

In the express train, after the precipitate actions and excitements of his flight and the border crossing, after the whirl of tensions and dangers, and still profoundly astonished that all had gone well, Friedrich Klein collapsed inwardly. Now that there was no longer any reason for haste the train seemed to him to be moving southward with a strange impetuousness, carrying its few passengers speedily past lakes, mountains, waterfalls, and other wonders of nature, through numbing tunnels and over gently swaying bridges. It was all foreign, beautiful, and rather meaningless, pictures from schoolbooks and postcards, landscapes remembered as seen before but really of no personal concern. So now he was in a foreign land where he would henceforth belong. There was no returning home. The money question had been settled; he had it with him, all in large bills safely stowed away in his breast pocket.

There was, in the back of his mind, the pleasant and reassuring thought that now nothing more could happen to him, that he was safely across the border and for the present protected by his false passport. He brought this thought repeatedly to the forefront of consciousness, craving to warm and satisfy himself with it; but this pretty thought was now like a dead bird that a child tries to revive by blowing on its wings. It was not alive, did not open its eye, fell like lead from the hand, gave no pleasure, had no glitter. It was strange, as he had noticed frequently during these past days, that he was far from being able to think what he pleased. He had no authority over his thoughts. They ran along as they wished, and do what he might they dwelt on ideas that tormented him.

It was as if his brain were a kaleidoscope in which the shifting images were directed by another's hand. Perhaps this was due only to his long spell of insomnia and agitation; his nerves had been bad for a considerable time. At any rate it was unpleasant, and if his mind did not manage to find its way soon to something like calm and joyousness, he would be desperate.

Friedrich Klein felt for the revolver in his coat pocket. That revolver was another of those items belonging to his new equipment, the new part he was playing, the mask he had donned. Really, how disgusting and bothersome it was to be dragging such stuff with him and to have to carry, down into his thin, poisoned sleep, all the rest: a crime, forged papers, money secretly sewn into his clothes, the revolver, the alias. It all had the savour of detective stories, of crude romanticism, and none of it corresponded to the image of Klein, the good fellow. It was disgusting and bothersome, and there was no sense of relief and liberation about it, such as he had hoped for.

Good Lord, why had he taken all this upon himself – he, a man of nearly forty, generally known as a hard-working civil servant and a quiet, harmless citizen with scholarly leanings, the father of adorable children? Why? He felt that something must have driven him to it, a compulsion sufficiently strong to lead a man like himself to attempt the impossible, and only when he knew, when he understood the nature of this compulsion and obsession, when he had restored order inside himself, would anything like peace of mind be possible.

With a violent effort he sat upright, pressed his temples with his thumbs, and made an effort to think. He was not very successful. His head was like glass, and hollowed out by agitation, fatigue, and lack of sleep. But there was no help for it, he must reflect. He must seek, and must find; he had to know that there was once again a centre inside himself. He had to understand himself at least to some degree. Otherwise life was no longer endurable.

Painfully, he tried to put together the memories of these past days. It was like picking up slivers of porcelain with pincers in order to glue together a broken snuffbox. There were nothing but fragments; none had any connection with any of the others; none indicated the structure and colour of the whole. What memories! He saw a small blue case from which he was taking, with trembling hand, his superior's official seal. He saw the old man at the teller's window cashing his cheque in brown and blue banknotes. He saw a telephone booth in which, while he spoke, he braced his left hand against the wall in order to keep himself from falling. Or rather, he did not really see himself. He saw a stranger doing all these things, a man whose name was Klein and who was not himself. He saw this man burning letters, writing letters. He saw him eating in a restaurant. He saw him – but no, that was not a stranger, that was he, that was Friedrich Klein himself! – stooped at night over the bed of a sleeping child. No, that had been himself! How that hurt, even now in memory. How it hurt to see the sleeping child's face and to hear his breathing and to know: never again would he see these dear eyes opening, never see this little mouth laughing and eating, never again be kissed by it. How that hurt! Why was this man Klein inflicting such hurts upon himself?

It was essential to pick up the little shards. The train stopped. A large, unfamiliar station lay outside the window. Doors banged, suit-cases swayed past the windows of the car. Blue and yellow signs pro-claimed loudly: Hotel Milano, Hotel Continental! Must he pay atten-tion to these things? Were they important? Was there any danger? He closed his eyes and for a minute sank into numbness, then started up again, rubbed his eyes until he could open them wide, played alert. Where was he? The station was still there. Stop – what is my name? For the thousandth time he tested himself. All right: What is my name? Klein. No, devil take it. Away with Klein. Klein no longer existed. He groped in his breast pocket, where he kept his passport.

How exhausting all this was. In fact, if people only knew how madly tiresome it is to be a criminal . . . ! He clenched his hands with the effort. None of this concerned him at all, Hotel Milano station, porters – he could just as well forget about all this. There was something else far more important. What was it?

Half dozing, with the train moving again, he returned to his thoughts. For it was terribly important; what was at stake was whether life was going to be endurable any longer. Or – wasn't it simpler to put an end to the whole wearisome nonsense? Didn't he have poison with him? The opium? Oh no, now he remembered, he had not been able to obtain the poison, of course. But he had the revolver. That was right. Very good. Fine.

He said 'very good' and 'fine' aloud under his breath, and added several words more. Suddenly he heard himself talking to himself, started, looked in the windowpane and saw his distorted face reflected, a stranger's, a sad, crazy mask of a face. Good Lord, he cried into his own depths, good Lord! What should he do? What was the point of living? He could smash his forehead into this pale mask, throw himself into this stupid, dirt-smeared pane, cut his throat with the glass, fall head-first on to the tracks, be rolled over by the droning, thundering wheels of all the cars, have everything wound up together around the wheels, guts and brains, bones and heart, eyes too – crushed along the tracks, reduced to nothing, erased. This was the only thing that could still be wished for, that still had meaning.

While he despairingly stared at his mirror image, and bumped his nose against the glass, he fell asleep again. Perhaps for seconds, perhaps for hours. His head swayed back and forth, but he did not open his eyes.

He awoke from a dream. The tail end of it remained in his memory. He was sitting, he had dreamed, in the front seat of an automobile that was moving rapidly and rather recklessly through a city, up and down hills. Beside him sat someone who was driving. In the dream he gave the driver a punch in the stomach, snatched the wheel from his hand, and now drove himself, drove wildly and terrifyingly over hill and dale, barely skirting horses and shop windows, grazing trees so closely that sparks flashed in his eyes.

He awoke from this dream. His head felt clearer. He smiled at the dream images. That punch in the stomach was good; he could still feel the glee of it. Now he began reconstructing the dream and thinking it over. How the car had whistled past the trees. Perhaps that came from the train? But driving himself had been, in spite of all the danger, a pleasure, a joy, a relief! Yes, it was better to drive yourself even if it meant peril than always to be driven and directed by others.

But in the dream, who was it he had hit? Who was the driver; who had been sitting beside him at the wheel of an automobile? He could not remember any face or shape, merely the feeling of someone else, a vague, obscure mood . . . Who could it have been? Someone he respected, whom he allowed to have power over his life, whom he bowed before yet secretly hated, and whom ultimately he punched in the stomach. Perhaps his father? Or one of his superiors? Or – or was it after all . . . ?

Klein opened his eyes wide. He had found one end of the lost thread. Now everything came back to him. The dream was forgotten. There were more important things. Now he knew! Now he was beginning to know, to guess, to sense, why he was sitting in this train, why his name was no longer Klein, why he had embezzled money and forged papers. At last, at last!

Yes, that was it. There was no longer any point concealing it from himself. It had all been done because of his wife, solely because of his wife. How good that he knew that at last.

From the high tower of this awareness he now suddenly thought he could see over vast stretches of his life that for a long time had seemed nothing but small, disconnected segments. He looked back upon a great long line, upon his whole marriage, and the distance traversed seemed to him a weary, dreary road on which a man toils alone through the dust bearing heavy burdens on his back. Somewhere far back, invisible now beyond the dust, he knew that the bright hills and rustling green tree-tops of youth had vanished. Yes, he had once been young, and no commonplace youth; he had dreamed great dreams, had asked much of life and of himself. But since then there had been nothing but dust and burdens, the long road, heat and weary legs, and a slumberous, ageing nostalgia lurking in his parching heart. That had been his life. That had been his life.

He looked out through the window and gave a start of amazement. The scenery was unfamiliar. Suddenly he realized that he was in the southland. Astonished, he straightened up and leaned forward. Once again a veil dropped away and the puzzle of his destiny became a little clearer to him. He was in the south! He saw grapevines on green terraces, golden-brown walls half in ruins, as in old engravings, and rosy blossoming trees. A small station fled past, with an Italian name, something with *ogno* or *ogna*.

Now Klein could read a part of the signpost of his destiny. He was leaving behind his marriage, his job, everything which had hitherto been life and homeland to him. And he was heading south. Only now did he realize why, in the midst of the daze and harassment of his flight, he had chosen as his destination that city with the Italian name. He had picked it out of a hotel list, seemingly at random; he might just as well have said Amsterdam, Zurich, or Malmö. But now it was no longer chance. He was in the south; he had crossed the Alps. And in doing this he had fulfilled the most glowing dream of his youth, that youth whose relics had vanished along the dreary road of a meaningless life. An unknown power had arranged matters so that the two most ardent desires of his life would be fulfilled: the long-forgotten yearning for the south, and the secret, never clearly formulated craving for escape and liberty from the serfdom and dust of his marriage. That quarrel with his superior, that wonderful chance to embezzle the money – all that, which had seemed so important to him, now shrank to a series of petty accidents. These were not what had guided him. Those two great desires in his soul had proved triumphant; the rest had been nothing but ways and means.

Faced with this new insight, Klein was startled. He felt like a child who has played with matches and set fire to a house. Now it was burning. Good Lord! And what was he getting out of it? Suppose he rode all the way to Sicily or Constantinople – would that make him twenty years younger?

Meanwhile the train rode on, and village after village came towards him, each of a foreign beauty, a gay picture book containing all the pretty features people expected of the south and knew from postcards: beautifully arched bridges over streams, brown cliffs, stone walls overgrown by small ferns, tall, slender campaniles, brightly painted church fronts, roofed marketplaces, lovely arches, rose-coloured houses and stout arcades painted the coolest blue, chestnut trees and here and there black cypresses, clambering goats, and on the lawn in front of a villa the first squat palms. Everything was remarkable and rather improbable, but all together it was most charming and promised something like consolation. This southland existed; it was no fable. The bridges and cypresses were youthful dreams realized. The houses and palm trees said: you are no longer in the old routine; something purely new is beginning. The air and the sunshine seemed spiced and stronger, breathing easier, life more possible, the revolver more dispensable, being erased upon the rails less urgent. In spite of everything, an effort seemed possible. Perhaps life could be endured.

Again exhaustion overcame him. This time he yielded more easily and slept until evening, when the resonant name of the city he had picked from the hotel list awakened him. Hastily, he left the train.

A man with 'Hotel Milano' blazoned on his cap addressed him in German. He reserved a room and took the address. Dazed with sleep, he reeled out of the glass-enclosed station into the soft evening.

'This is rather the way I imagined Honolulu,' he thought. A fantastically charged landscape, with night falling, swayed towards him, strange and incomprehensible. The hill dropped away steeply in front of him; far below were the staggered houses of the city. He looked vertically down into illuminated squares. A crescent of steep sugarloaf hills plunged down into a lake whose dark waters reflected the innumerable quayside lights. A cog railway train dropped like a basket down the shaft to the town, looking half dangerous, half toylike. On some of the high hillsides illuminated windows glowed in whimsical rows all the way to the peak, patterned in ladder steps and constellations. From the town loomed the roofs of large hotels; amid them were dusky gardens. A warm, summery evening breeze, full of dust and scents, blew pleasantly beneath the brilliant street lights. From the tangle of lights about the dark lake, band music floated upward, the rhythm firm, the sound preposterous.

Whether this was Honolulu, Mexico, or Italy really should not matter to him. It was a strange land; it was a new world and new air; and although it confused him and produced a secret anxiety, yet it bore the savour of intoxication and forgetfulness and new, untried emotions.

A street seemed to lead out into open country. He strolled along it, past sheds and empty trucks, then past small suburban houses where loud voices were shouting in Italian and a mandolin was clinking in the yard of a tavern. In the last house along the street a girl's voice rang out; the sweetness of it tugged at his heart. To his delight he was able to understand many of the words, and he noted the refrain:

> *Mamma non vuole, papà ne meno,*
> *Come faremo a fare l'amor?*

It was as if it had come from the dreams of his youth. Utterly absorbed, he walked on down the street, ecstatically merging with the warm night loud with the chirp of crickets. He came to a vineyard and stopped, enchanted: fireworks, a multitude of miniature glowing greenish sparks filled the air and the tall fragrant grass. A thousand shooting stars reeled in a drunken dance. It was a swarm of fireflies slowly and noiselessly flitting through the warmly quivering night. The summery air and earth seemed to be exulting fantastically in luminescent figures and a thousand tiny wheeling constellations.

For a long time the foreigner stood yielding to the enchantment, forgetful of the painful story of his journey and the painful story of his life. Did any reality still exist? Were there such things as businesses and police? Magistrates and market reports? Was there a railroad station ten minutes' walk from this spot?

Slowly the fugitive, who had travelled out of his life and into a fairy tale, turned back towards the city. Street lamps came to glowing life. People called out to him words he did not understand. Huge, unfamiliar trees stood hung with blossom. A stone church thrust its escarpment out over an abyss. Bright streets pierced by staircases flowed swiftly as mountain brooks down into the town.

Klein found his hotel. And as he entered the over-bright, banal lobby and stairwell, his intoxication vanished and his anxious timidity returned, his curse and his mark of Cain. Uneasily, he skulked past the sharp, appraising eyes of the concierge, the waiters, the elevator boy, and the other hotel guests and made his way into the dreariest corner of a restaurant. In a faint voice he asked for the menu, and as if he were still poor and had to be thrifty, he took careful stock of the prices of all the dishes, ordered something cheap, tried the artificial cheer of a half bottle of Bordeaux from which he had no pleasure, and was grateful when he was at last lying behind a locked door in his small, shabby room. Soon he fell asleep, slept deep and greedily, but only for two or three hours. It was still the middle of the night when he awoke again.

Emerging from the abysses of the unconscious, he stared into the hostile blackness, not knowing where he was, guiltily oppressed by the feeling of having forgotten and neglected something important. Groping confusedly, he felt for a switch and turned on the light. The small room burst into glaring light, alien, dreary, and meaningless. Where was he? The plush chairs stared malignantly. Everything had a cold and challenging look. He caught a glimpse of himself in the mirror and read in his face what he had forgotten. Yes, he knew. He had formerly not had this face, these eyes, these wrinkles, this flesh. It was a new face; he had already noticed that once before, in the mirror of a windowpane at some point in the harried drama of these insane days. It was not his good, quiet, rather long-suffering Friedrich Klein face. It was the face of a marked man, stamped by destiny with new symbols, both older and younger than the former face, like a mask and yet permeated by a strange inner glow. No one loved such a face.

Here he sat in a hotel room in the southland, with his marked face. At home the children he had abandoned were sleeping. He would never again see them sleeping, never see them just awakening, never again hear their voices. Never again would he drink from the glass of water on that night table beside the floor lamp, the table on which lay the evening newspaper and a book, and on the wall above the head of the bed the pictures of his parents, and everything, everything. Instead, here he was in a foreign hotel staring into the mirror, into the sad and anxious face of Klein the criminal, and the plush furniture stared back, cold and nasty, and everything was different, nothing was right any more. If his father had lived to see this! . . .

Never since his youth had Klein been left so starkly and so solitarily to his emotions. Never had he been exposed so utterly to alien surroundings, been so naked beneath the sharp, inexorable sunlight of fate. He had always been busy with something, with something other than himself; he had always had things to do and to be worried about, money, promotion, the peace of the household, school matters, and children's illnesses. The imposing, sacred duties of the citizen, the husband, the father had always loomed over him. He had lived in their shade and shelter, made sacrifices to them, derived the justification and meaning of his life from them. Now he was suddenly suspended naked in space, confronting sun and moon alone, and he felt that the air was icy and rarefied.

And the strange part of it was that no earthquake had thrust him into this fearful and dangerous predicament, no god or devil, but he himself, he alone! His own act had sent him hurtling here, had set him down in the midst of this alien infinity. Everything had arisen within himself; his destiny had grown to maturity in his own heart. Out of it had come crime and rebellion, the flouting of sacred obligations, the leap into space, hatred for his wife, flight, loneliness and perhaps suicide. Others no doubt had experienced loss and upheaval through fire and warfare, through accidents and the ill will of others. But he, Klein the criminal, could not ascribe anything to outside agencies, could not clear himself, could not make others responsible – or perhaps at most his wife. Yes, she certainly must be cited, she made responsible; he could point to her if ever an accounting were demanded of him.

A great rage flared up within him, and suddenly he remembered something, burning and deadly, a clump of emotions and experiences. It reminded him of the dream of the automobile and of the punch in the stomach he had given his enemy.

What he remembered now was a feeling or a fantasy, a strange and morbid psychological state, a temptation, an insane craving, or whatever was the proper name for it. It was the conception or vision of a terrible murder he was committing, killing his wife, his children, and himself. Several times, he now recalled, while the mirror continued to show him his branded, distraught criminal's face, several times he had been forced to imagine this fourfold murder, or rather he had desperately fended off this wild and horrible vision, as it had then seemed to him. At those very times the thoughts, dreams, and torments had begun within him which, he now believed, had led by and by to the embezzlement and his flight. Perhaps – it was possible – not just the growing and ultimately intense dislike for his wife and his marital life had driven him from home, but even more the fear that one day he might after all commit this far more dreadful crime: might kill them all, slaughter them, and see them lying in their blood. And there was more to it: this fantasy too had its background. It had come to him now and then like a slight dizzy spell that makes you think you must let go and drop to the floor. But the vision, the image of the murders in his mind, sprang from a particular source. Incredible that he was only realizing that now.

At the time, when the obsessional idea of killing his family had first gripped him, and he had been frightened to death by this diabolical vision, a trivial recollection had come to him, as if to mock him. It was this: years ago, when his life was still harmless, almost happy, he and some office associates had begun discussing the horrible crime of a south German schoolteacher named W (he could not recall the name right off) who had butchered his entire family in a horribly bloody way and then taken his own life. The question had been raised to what extent a man who did such a thing was responsible for his actions and whether there was any understanding and explaining such an act, such a gruesome explosion of human atrociousness. The subject had upset Klein greatly, and when one of his associates had attempted to give a psychological explanation of the killing, Klein had exclaimed with extreme vehemence that faced with such an atrocious crime the only possible attitude for a decent man was outrage and abhorrence; such a deed could be conceived only in the brain of a devil, and no punishment, no tribunal, no torture could be harsh enough for a criminal of this type. He still recalled precisely the table at which they had been sitting, and the astounded, somewhat critical look with which that older associate had glanced at him after this outburst.

Later, when he for the first time saw himself lost in a hideous fantasy of being the murderer of his family, and had shuddered away from the thought, he had at once recollected that discussion about the murderer W, although it had taken place years before. And strangely, although he could have sworn that at the time he had expressed his truest feelings with complete sincerity, there was now an ugly inner voice mockingly calling out to him: even then, even then, years ago, during the talk about the schoolteacher W, you understood his act in your heart, understood and approved it, and your outrage and agitation sprang only from your own philistine, hypocritical refusal to admit what you really knew inwardly. Those terrible punishments and tortures he had wished upon the murderer, the outrage with which he had reviled the man's act, had really been directed against himself, against the germ of crime which undoubtedly had been present in him at the time. His intense agitation throughout this whole incident had its source solely in the fact that he saw himself in prison, accused of the murders, and that he was trying to salve his conscience by invoking on himself the charge and the verdict. As if by flaying himself he could punish or drive out the secret criminality within his own being.

Klein reached this point in his thoughts, and felt that something terribly important for him was involved, in fact life itself. But it was inexpressibly toilsome to unravel these memories and thoughts and to put them into some kind of order. A faint forewarning of ultimate, redeeming insights underlay his fatigue and his horror for his whole situation. He got up, washed his face, and paced barefoot back and forth until he was shivering with cold and thought that now he would sleep.

But no sleep came. He lay in bed, inescapably the victim of his memories, of ugly, painful, and humiliating feelings: hatred for his wife, pity for himself, perplexity, a craving for explanations, excuses, consolations. And since no consolations occurred to him and the way to understanding was so deeply and mercilessly hidden in the secret, dangerous thickets of his memories, and sleep still would not come, he lay for the rest of the night in a state of agony worse than anything he had hitherto known. All the horrible feelings that contended within him combined into a dreadful, suffocating, deadly anxiety, a nightmarish pressure upon his heart and lungs. It increased again and again to the very edge of his endurance. He had long known what anxiety was, had known it for years, and more than ever in the past few weeks and days. But never before had he felt it gripping his throat so fiercely. Compulsively, he was forced to think of the most trivial things, a forgotten key, the hotel bill, and to build mountains of cares and painful problems out of them. The question of whether this shabby little room for the night was likely to cost more than three and a half francs, and whether in that case he ought to stay on in the hotel, kept him breathless, sweating, and with pounding heart for about an hour. Yet he knew all the while how stupid these thoughts were and repeatedly talked to himself reasonably and reassuringly as to a defiant child, reckoning out on his fingers the utter insubstantiality of his worries – in vain, totally in vain. Rather, something like cruel mockery gleamed even behind these cajoleries and attempts at self-comfort, as though the whole thing were mere make-believe, just like his make-believe over the murderer W. It was quite clear to him that his deathly fear, his ghastly sense of strangulation and condemnation, could not come from his worry over a few francs or any similar causes. Worse, more serious matters lurked behind this – but what? They must be things connected with the murderous school-teacher, with his own cravings to kill, and with all the sickness and disorder within him. But how could he get at it? How find the bottom? There was not a spot inside him that was not bleeding, nothing that was not sick and rotten and insanely sensitive to pain. He felt that he could not bear this much longer. If it went on, and if many other nights like this followed, he would go mad or take his life.

Tensely, he sat up in bed and tried to drain utterly his sense of his predicament, in order to be done with it once and for all. But it was always the same. Alone and helpless, he sat with fevered brow and painful pressure around his head, gripped by a fear of fate which held him spellbound like a bird watching a snake. Fate, he now knew, did not come from just anywhere; it grew within himself. If he found no remedy for it, it would consume him. Anxiety, this horrible anxiety, would pursue him, would dog his every step, would drive him farther and farther from rationality, until he reached the brink. Already he could feel how close the brink was.

If only he could understand – that might mean salvation. He was still far from grasping his predicament and what had led up to it. So far he had made no more than a beginning; his feelings told him that clearly. If he could pull himself together and sum up everything precisely, arrange and consider all that had taken place, perhaps he would find the thread. The whole would acquire meaning and outline and might then be endurable. But this effort, this last struggle to pull himself together, was too much for him. It exceeded his strength. He simply was not up to it. The more strenuously he tried to think, the more he bungled it. Instead of memories and explanations he found only empty holes within himself. Nothing came to him, while once again he was overwhelmed by the feeling that he might have forgotten the one most important thing. He poked and probed around inside himself like a nervous traveller who fumbles through all his pockets and suitcases for his ticket, which he possibly has tucked into his hat, or is even holding in his hand. But what good did that 'possibly' do?

Earlier, perhaps an hour or more ago, had he not had an insight, made a find? What had it been? What? It was gone; he could not locate it again. Despairingly, he struck his forehead with his fist. God in heaven, let me find the key! Let me not die this way, so wretchedly, so stupidly, so sadly! Torn to tatters like drifting clouds in a storm, his whole past flew by him, millions of images tangled and intertwined, unrecognizable and mocking, yet each one reminding him of something. Of what, of what?

Suddenly he found the name 'Wagner' on his lips. As if unconscious he spoke it aloud: 'Wagner – Wagner.' Where did the name come from? From what shaft within himself? What was it driving at? Who was Wagner? Wagner?

He hung on to the name. He had a task, a problem, and that was better than floating in formlessness. All right: Who is Wagner? What concern of mine is Wagner? Why are my lips, these twisted lips in my criminal's face, murmuring the name Wagner here in the middle of the night? He pulled himself together. All sorts of notions came into his mind. He thought of Lohengrin, and then of his somewhat ambiguous feelings about the composer Richard Wagner. At the age of twenty he had been wild about him. Later he had grown wary, and in time had accumulated a number of reservations and doubts on the subject. He had done a great deal of criticizing of Wagner, and perhaps these criticisms were directed less towards Richard Wagner than to his own former love for the composer's music? Ha, had he caught himself again? Had he uncovered another fraud, a small lie, a minor crime? Oh yes, one thing after another was coming to light. In the irreproachable life of Friedrich Klein, husband and civil servant, things had not at all been so irreproachable, not at all so clear. There was a skeleton hidden in every closet. Yes, of course, that was the case with Wagner too. Friedrich Klein had taken a very strong line against the composer Richard Wagner. Why? Because Friedrich Klein could not forgive himself for having raved about this same Wagner as a young man. In Wagner he was persecuting his own youthful enthusiasm, his own youth, his own love. Why? Because youth and artistic enthusiasm and Wagner and all the rest reminded him painfully of things he had lost, because he had let himself be married by a woman he did not love, or at any rate not in the right way, not sufficiently. Oh yes, and as he behaved towards Wagner he had in his official capacity behaved towards many persons and things. He was such a decent fellow, Herr Klein, and behind his decency he was concealing nothing but filth and iniquity. If he had tried to be honest – how many secret thoughts had he hidden from himself? How many glances at pretty girls in the street, how much envy of loving couples whom he encountered in the evenings when he walked home from his office? And then the thoughts of murder. And had he not turned the hatred which he should have directed towards himself against that schoolteacher —

He started suddenly. One more connection! The schoolteacher and murderer had – why, of course, his name had been Wagner. So there was the crux of it. Wagner – that was the name of that madman who had killed his whole family. Hadn't his entire life for years been somehow connected with this man Wagner? Hadn't that evil shadow pursued him everywhere?

Well, thank God he had found the thread again. Oh yes, and once upon a time, in long-past, better days, he had savagely denounced this man Wagner and called down the cruelest punishments upon his head. Yet he himself had later, without thinking of Wagner, had the same thought and had several times seen himself in a kind of vision killing his wife and his children.

And was that not perfectly understandable after all? Was it not right? Was it so very difficult to see that the responsibility for the existence of children could become intolerable to a man, as intolerable as his own nature and own being, which he regarded as sheer error, as nothing but torture and guilt?

With a sigh, he thought this thought through to the end. It now appeared quite certain that even then, when he first heard about it, he had understood Wagner's killings in his heart and had approved of them, approved of them only as a possibility, of course. Even then, when he did not yet feel unhappy and regard his life as a mess, even then, years ago, when he still thought he loved his wife and believed in her love for him, even then his inner nature had understood the schoolteacher Wagner and had secretly concurred with his horrible act of butchery. What he said at the time had expressed only the opinion of his intellect, not that of his heart. His heart, that innermost root from which his destiny sprang, had for ever and ever held a different opinion. It had understood and approved crimes. There had always been two Friedrich Kleins, one visible and one secret, a civil servant and a criminal, a paterfamilias and a murderer.

But in those days he had always been on the side of his 'better' self, the civil servant and decent person, the husband and upright citizen. He had never condoned the secret intentions of his heart, had never even recognized them. And yet that inner voice had been secretly guiding him and finally made of him a fugitive and outcast.

Gratefully, he clung to this thought. It was at least an element of consistency, something approaching rationality. It was not yet enough; everything important still remained obscure; but he had achieved a certain amount of light, a modicum of truth. And truth was what mattered. If only he did not again lose the end of the thread.

Between waking and sleep, feverish with exhaustion, poised on the brink between thought and dream, he lost the thread again a hundred times, found it anew a hundred times. Until day broke and the noise of the streets sounded in through his window.

Chapter Two

In the course of the morning Klein tramped through the city. He came to a hotel whose garden he liked, went in, looked at rooms, and took one. Only as he was departing did he note the name of the hotel. He read: Hotel Continental. Wasn't this name familiar to him? Had it not been prophesied? Just like the Hotel Milano? But he soon gave up searching his memory and was content with the atmosphere of foreignness, playfulness, and peculiar portentousness into which he seemed to have stumbled.

The magic of the day before gradually returned. It was very good that he was in the south, he thought gratefully. He had been guided well. Were it not for this charming enchantment all around him, which promoted this calm sauntering and self-forgetfulness, he would have been entirely at the mercy of his compulsive thoughts with all the suffering they entailed. But as it was, he succeeded in vegetating in pleasant fatigue for hours at a time, without compulsions, without anxiety, without thoughts. That did him good. It was fortunate that this southland existed, and that he had prescribed it for himself. The south made life easier. It comforted. It anaesthetized.

Even now, in broad daylight, the landscape looked fantastic and improbable. The mountains were all too close, too steep, too high, as if envisioned by some eccentric painter. But everything near and small was lovely: a tree, a patch of lake shore, a house painted in gay colours, a garden wall, a narrow strip of wheat among the grapes, small and tended as a kitchen garden. All this was charming and amiable, gay and sociable; it breathed haleness and trustfulness. This small, amiable, hospitable landscape with its serenely cheerful people was something you could love. And something to love – what a salvation!

With a passionate determination to forget and to lose himself, the sufferer in flight from lurking anxieties immersed himself in this foreign world. He walked out into the open country, country of attractive, industriously tended farmlands. Neither the peasants nor their lands reminded him of the farms of his own country, but rather of Homer and the Romans; there was something age-old, cultivated and yet primitive, about this landscape. It had an innocence and a maturity lacking in the north. The small chapels and shrines, brightly painted and gently crumbling, most often adorned with bouquets of wild flowers brought by children, stood everywhere along the roads in honour of saints. They seemed to him to have the same meaning and to derive from the same spirit as the many small sanctuaries of the ancients which honoured a divinity in every grove, spring, and mountain. There was a serene piety about them that smelled of bread and wine and health.

He turned back to the town, walked under echoing arcades, tired himself out on rough cobblestone pavements, peered curiously into open stores and workshops, bought Italian newspapers without reading them, and finally, thoroughly tired, found himself in a splendid lakeside park. Tourists were strolling about or sitting on benches reading, and tremendous old trees hung like dark vaults above blackish-green water, as if infatuated with their reflections. A host of improbable plants, smoke tree and snakewood, cork oaks and other rarities, dotted the lawns, their shapes rakish or anxious or sorrowful. There were flowers everywhere. And on the distant shore across the lake glimmered, white and pink, lovely villages and country houses.

He was sitting hunched on a bench, almost on the point of nodding off, when a firm, elastic footstep startled him into wakefulness. A woman, a girl, passed by him. She was wearing russet-coloured laced boots and a short skirt above flimsy net stockings. She walked vigorously, with a firm rhythm, erect and provocative. Proudly fashionable, she had a cool face with crimsoned lips and wore her golden hair piled high. For just a second in passing her glance fell upon him with that self-assured, appraising look of doormen and hotel bellboys. Indifferently, she walked on.

Certainly, Klein thought, she is right; I am not a person to be noticed. A girl like that doesn't look twice at my sort. Nevertheless, the brevity and coolness of her glance secretly pained him. He felt deprecated and despised by someone who saw only the surface, and from the depths of his past he summoned up weapons to arm himself against her. Already he had forgotten that her fine, lively shoes, her firm elastic gait, her taut leg in the thin silk stocking had for a moment fascinated him and given him pleasure. The rustling of her dress was extinguished, and the faint fragrance of her hair and skin. Cast away and crushed underfoot was the lovely breath of sex and the possibility of love that had come from her and just grazed him. Instead many memories rose up. How often he had seen such creatures, such young, self-assured, and provocative females, whether sluts or vain society women; how often their shameless provocation had irritated him, their self-assurance annoyed him, their cool, bold display of themselves repelled him. How often, on outings and in city restaurants, he had sincerely shared his wife's outrage at such unwomanly and hetaera-like creatures.

Crossly, he stretched out his legs. The woman had spoiled his good humour. He felt irritable and at a disadvantage. He knew that if this yellow-haired creature passed by once more and scrutinized him again, he would flush and decide that his clothes, his hat, his shoes, his face, his hair and beard were inadequate and inferior. The devil take her. That yellow hair alone! It was false; nowhere in the world was real hair so yellow. And she wore cosmetics, too. How anyone could so lower herself as to smear lipstick on her lips – negroid! And such people went about as if the world belonged to them; they had that manner, that assurance, that brazenness, and took the joy out of life for decent persons.

Along with the newly roiling emotions of displeasure, vexation, and constraint another great bubble of the past simmered to the surface, and suddenly another insight: these are your wife's views you are invoking. You are setting her up as judge, you are subordinating yourself to her again! For a moment there washed over him a feeling that could perhaps be defined as: I am an ass for still counting myself among 'decent people'; I am no longer one, of course; I belong just as much as this yellow-haired girl to a world which is no longer my former world, and no longer the decent world. It is one where decent and indecent no longer mean anything, where everyone is trying to live through this difficult life on his own. For the space of a moment he felt that his contempt for the yellow-haired girl was just as superficial and insincere as his one-time condemnation of Wagner the murderer, and his distaste for the other Wagner whose music he had felt to be too sensual. For a second his buried understanding, his lost self, opened its eyes and told him with its omniscient gaze that all indignation, all condemnation, all

contempt were mistaken and childish and rebounded upon the poor
devil who did the despising.

This good, omniscient understanding told him also that he was again
confronting a mystery whose proper interpretation was important for
his life, that this slut or demimondaine, this scent of elegance, seduction,
and sex, was by no means repugnant and insulting to him. Rather, that
he was only imagining such judgements and had hammered them into
his mind out of fear of his real nature, out of fear of Wagner, out of fear
of the animal or devil he might discover if he ever threw off the fetters
and disguises of his moralistic respectability. Something akin to mocking laughter abruptly flared up within him, but soon subsided. The
feeling of displeasure won out again. It was uncanny the way every
awakening, every emotion, every thought infallibly struck him precisely
where he was weak and only too susceptible to torments. Now he was
caught up in his weakness once more and brooding over his misspent
life, his wife, his crime, the hopelessness of his future. Anxiety returned;
the omniscient ego sank beneath the surface like an unheard sigh. Oh,
what agony! No, the yellow-haired girl was not to blame for this. And
all the intense feelings he had directed against her did her no harm, of
course; they struck only himself.

He got up and began walking. In the past he had often thought he was
leading a fairly solitary life, and with a measure of vanity had ascribed
this to a certain resigned philosophic quality in himself. Among his
associates, moreover, he had the reputation of being a scholar, reader,
and secret intellectual. Good Lord, he had never been solitary! He had
talked with his associates, with his wife, with his children, with all sorts
of people, and such talk had made the days pass and his cares bearable.
Even when he had been alone, it had been no sort of solitude. He had
shared the opinions, anxieties, joys, and comforts of many others, of a
whole world. Community had always been all around him and had
penetrated deep into him, and even in solitude, in suffering and in
resignation, he had always belonged to a group, a protective association,
the world of decent, righteous, and respectable people. But now, now
he was tasting loneliness. Every arrow struck him directly, every reason
for comfort proved pointless, every escape from anxiety only led back
into that world with which he had broken, which had broken him and
slipped away from him. Everything that had been good and right all his
life was no longer good and right. He had to draw everything out of himself now. Nobody was helping him. And what did he find inside himself? Nothing but disorder and dissension.

An automobile came towards him, and as he stepped out of the way it diverted his thoughts, threw new fodder to them. In his head he felt the giddiness and emptiness of insomnia. 'Automobile,' he thought, or said the word under his breath, not knowing what it meant. Closing his eyes for a moment after an onrush of weakness, he saw a picture that seemed familiar, that reminded him of something and infused new blood into his thoughts. He saw himself sitting at the wheel of a car and steering it. That was a dream he had once dreamed. In the dream-feeling that he had knocked the driver down and seized the wheel himself there had been something like liberation and triumph. There was comfort there somewhere, though hard to find. But it was there. If only in fantasy or in dream there was the sweet possibility of guiding his vehicle all by himself, of knocking any other driver off the seat with mocking laughter, and even if the vehicle thereafter acted capriciously, drove over sidewalks or into houses and people, it was still a delicious thing to do and far better than being sheltered and riding under the tutelage of others, remaining a child for ever.

A child? He had to smile. The recollection came that as a child and young man he had hated and cursed his name Klein because it meant 'small'. Now that was no longer his name. Was that not important – a symbol, a parable? He had ceased to be small and a child; he would no longer let himself be led around by others.

In the hotel he had a good mild wine with his meal; he had ordered the wine at random, but noted its name. There were few things that helped you, few that comforted and made life easier; it was important to know what these few things were. This wine was one such, and the southern air and landscape another. What else? Were there more? Yes, thinking was another of those comforting things that did you good and helped you live. But not all kinds of thinking. Oh no, there was a way of thinking that was torture and madness. There was a way of thinking that was a pawing over of what could not be changed and led to nothing but disgust, worry, and surfeit with life. What you had to seek and learn was a different kind of thinking. Was it a form of thinking at all? It was a condition, an inner state, which could last only for moments and was spoiled by strenuous efforts to think. In this highly desirable state you had inspirations, memories, visions, fantasies, insights of a special kind. The thought (or dream) of the automobile was of that good and comforting kind, and so was the sudden memory of Wagner the killer and of that discussion about him years ago. The curious insight about the name Klein was another. When you had such thoughts, such inspirations, the anxiety receded for a few moments and the horrible sense of nausea gave way to a rapid flash of security. Then the feeling came that all was well, that loneliness was proud and strong, the past overcome, the near future without terrors.

This was something he had to grasp, something he had to teach himself. His salvation lay in such thoughts, in finding his way to them, in evoking them from himself and cultivating them. He pondered and pondered. He did not know how he had passed the afternoon; the hours melted away as if in sleep, and perhaps he actually had slept – who could tell. Again and again his thoughts circled around that mystery. He thought hard and long about his encounter with the yellow-haired girl. What did she mean? How was it that this brief episode, that momentary exchange of glances with an alien, beautiful, but reprehensible woman should for long hours have become the source of thoughts, feelings, excitements, memories, self-torments, indictments? How was it? Did this sort of thing happen to others also? Why had her figure, her walk, her leg, her shoes and stockings delighted him for the fraction of a moment? And then why had her coolly appraising look so severely disillusioned him? Why had that annoying look not merely disillusioned him and shaken him from his brief, erotic enchantment, but also insulted, offended, and devalued him to himself? Why had he opposed that glance with words and memories that belonged entirely to his former world, that no longer had any meaning? Why had he adduced reasons he no longer believed in? He had summoned up his wife's judgements, his colleagues' words, his former self's thoughts and opinions, the ideas of the respectable citizen and official he no longer was, to attack that yellow-haired woman and her scathing glance. He had felt the need to use every conceivable means to justify himself in the face of that glance, and he should have realized that all his means were a heap of old coins that would no longer pass for currency. And all these painful, protracted considerations had yielded nothing but heavy spirits, uneasiness, and painful feelings of his own wrongness. But for a single moment he had felt that other, so intensely desirable condition; for a moment he had inwardly shaken his head over all these painful considerations and had known better. He had known, for just a second, this: My thoughts about the yellow-haired girl are stupid and unworthy. She is as subject to fate as I am. God loves her as he loves me.

Whence had this sweet voice come? Where could he find it again, how coax it to return? On what branch was this rare, shy bird perched?

This voice spoke the truth, and truth was a blessing, was healing and refuge. This voice arose when he was at one with destiny in his own heart and when he loved himself; it was God's voice, or else it was the voice of his truest, innermost self, beyond all lies, apologies, and farces.

Why could he not hear this voice all the time? Why did truth always fly past him like a phantom that is only half glimpsed as it scurries by, and vanishes when you look straight at it? Why did he repeatedly see this gateway to happiness standing open, and why did it swing shut in his face whenever he wanted to enter?

In his room, awakening from a doze, he reached for a small volume of Schopenhauer that lay on his night table. He usually took the book with him on travels. He opened it at random and read a sentence: 'Whenever we look back upon the portion of life's road we have traversed, and when we fix our gaze upon our unfortunate steps in particular, along with their consequences, we often do not understand how we were able to do this or omit that; so that it appears as if an alien power guided our steps. Goethe says in *Egmont*: Man thinks he directs his life, leads himself; but his innermost being is irresistibly drawn in the direction of his destiny.' Was there not something here that concerned him? Something intimately connected with his thoughts today? Avidly he read on, but nothing more came; the subsequent lines and sentences left him unmoved. He laid the book aside, looked at his watch, found that he had forgotten to wind it and it had run down. Getting up, he looked out of the window. It seemed to be nearly evening.

He felt somewhat wearied as after intense intellectual effort, but he was not unpleasantly and futilely exhausted. Rather, this fatigue was meaningful, like that which follows satisfying work. I suppose I slept an hour or more, he thought, and went over to the mirror to brush his hair. He felt strangely easy and good, and in the mirror he saw himself smiling. His pale, over-strained face, which for so long he had seen distorted and rigid and wild, wore a gentle, amiable, good smile. Astonished, he shook his head and smiled at himself.

He went downstairs. At a few tables in the restaurant some people were already at their supper. Hadn't he just eaten? No matter, in any case he felt intensely eager to do so again, at once. Addressing lively queries to the waiter, he ordered a good meal.

'Would you care to ride to Castiglione this evening, sir?' the waiter asked as he served. 'There is a hotel motorboat leaving.'

Klein shook his head. No, such outings were not for him. Castiglione? He had already heard some talk about the place. It was an amusement area with a casino, a kind of small Monte Carlo. Good Lord, what would he do there?

While the coffee was being served, he took a small white rose from the bouquet in the crystal vase on the table and tucked it into his lapel. From the next table the smoke of a newly lit cigar drifted past him. Right, he wanted a good cigar too.

Indecisively, he walked back and forth in front of the hotel for a while. He felt a strong desire to return to that rural area where he had heard the Italian girl singing last night and, watching the magical sparkling dance of the fireflies, had for the first time sensed the sweet reality of the south. But he was also drawn to the park, to the still water under leafy shade, to the strange trees, and if the woman with the yellow hair had met him again her cold glance would not irritate or shame him now. Altogether – how unimaginably long a time had passed since yesterday! How much at home he already felt in this southland. How much he had experienced, thought, learned.

He strolled a block away from the hotel, wrapped in a good, gentle, summer evening breeze. Moths circled passionately around the street lamps as they winked on. Hard-working people belatedly closed their shops and fastened the shutters in front of them. Many children were still playing about, running among the small tables of the sidewalk cafés where coffee and lemonade were being drunk. An image of the Virgin in a wall niche smiled in the glow of burning candles. The benches by the lake were also still animated; people were laughing, quarrelling, singing, and here and there on the water a boat still bobbed, with shirtsleeved rowers and girls in white blouses.

Klein easily found the way back to the park, but the high gate was closed. Behind the tall iron bars stood the alien, silent darkness of the trees, already full of night and sleep. He looked in for a long time. Then he smiled, and only now did he become conscious of the secret wish that had impelled him to seek out this place outside the locked iron gate. Well, it did not matter; he could manage without the park, too.

On a bench by the lake he sat peaceably, watching people pass. In the bright light from the street lamp he unfolded an Italian newspaper and tried to read it. He did not understand everything, but each sentence he was able to translate gave him pleasure. It was a while before he began reaching beyond the grammar and paying attention to the sense. Then he found, with a certain astonishment, that the article was a violent, embittered denunciation of his people and his native country. How odd, he thought, all this is still going on. The Italians were writing about his nation just as his home newspapers had always done about Italy, exactly as censorious, exactly as indignant, exactly as convinced of the rightness of their own nation and the wrongness of the foreigners. It was also strange that this newspaper with its hatred and its cruel opinions did not manage to excite him. Or did it, in some measure? No, what was the point of indignation? All that was the manner and the language of a world to which he no longer belonged. It might be the better world, the right world – but it was no longer his.

He left the newspaper on the bench and walked on. Above profusely flowering rose bushes in a garden, a hundred coloured lights shone. People were entering; he joined them. A ticket seller, attendants, a wall with posters. In the middle of the garden was a hall without walls, merely a large canvas roof about which the innumerable coloured lights were draped. Many half-occupied garden tables filled the airy hall. In the background, glistening silver, green, and pink, too bright under the many lights, was a small raised stage. Below the platform sat musicians, a small orchestra. Lightly soaring, the flute breathed out into the many-hued warm night, the oboe swelled full-throatedly, the cello sang darkly, warmly, and bashfully. On the stage an old man was singing comic songs; forced laughter issued from his painted mouth; the rush of light was reflected from his worried bald pate.

Klein had not been expecting anything of the sort. For a moment he felt a sense of disappointment and criticism, and his old timidity about sitting alone in the midst of a well-clad lively crowd. The artificial joviality seemed to him to harmonize ill with the evening fragrance of the garden. But he sat down anyhow, and the light dripping from so many coloured bulbs soon reconciled him to the scene. It hung like a magic veil over the enclosure. Frail and deeply felt, the trivial music eddied towards him, mingled with the scent of all the roses. People sat about enjoying themselves. Above the tables, bottles, and cups of sherbet, gently powdered by the coloured lights, floated bright faces and vivid women's hats, and even the yellow and pink sherbets in the cups and the glasses of green and yellow lemonade harmonized like jewellery with the whole picture.

No one was listening to the comedian. The wretched old man stood lonely and ignored on his stage, singing what he had learned, the gem-like light pouring down on his unhappy figure. He ended his song and seemed relieved to have discharged his duty. Two or three persons at the front tables clapped. The singer walked off and soon reappeared in the garden; he took a seat at one of the tables near the orchestra. A young woman poured soda water into a glass for him, half rising as she did so. Klein looked over at her. It was the girl with the yellow hair.

Now, from somewhere, a shrill bell rang long and insistently. The crowd stirred. Many went out without their hats or coats. The table by the orchestra emptied also; the yellow-haired girl bustled out with the others, her hair gleaming brightly even outside the area under the lights. Only the old singer remained sitting at the table.

Klein gave himself a push and went over to the man. He politely greeted the old fellow, who merely nodded.

'Could you tell me what the bell means?' Klein asked.

'Intermission,' the comedian said.

'And where has everybody gone?'

'To gamble. There's a half-hour intermission, and they can play in the casino across the street.'

'Thank you. I didn't know there was a casino here too.'

'Not worth mentioning. Baby stuff. The highest stake is five francs.'

'Thank you very much.'

He tipped his hat again and turned around. Then it occurred to him that he could ask the old man about the girl with the yellow hair, with whom he stood on some familiar terms.

He hesitated, hat still in his hand. Then he walked away. What did he really want? Why should the girl concern him? But he sensed that she nevertheless did. It was only shyness, some delusion, an inhibition. A faint wave of annoyance rose in him, like a tenuous cloud. Melancholy was welling up again; now he was caught once more, unfree and annoyed with himself. It would be better for him to go home to the hotel. What was he doing here, among these pleasure-seekers? He was not one of them.

A waiter asking payment interrupted his thoughts. He became angry.

'Can't you wait until I call you?'

'Sorry, sir, I thought you wanted to leave. It comes out of my own pocket if someone runs off.'

He gave a larger tip than was necessary.

As he started to leave, he saw the yellow-haired girl returning. He lingered, and let her pass him. She walked erect, with lithe, light step, as if on springs. Her eyes met his, coolly, without recognition. He saw her face in bright light, a tranquil and sensible face, firm and pale, slightly blasé, her rouged mouth blood-red, grey, alert eyes, a pretty, finely-moulded ear on which a greenish oblong stone flashed. Her dress was of white silk; her slender neck descended into opal shadow. She wore a thin necklace of green stones.

He looked at her, secretly excited, and again with divided feelings. Something about her lured him, spoke of happiness and intimacy, was redolent of flesh and hair and groomed beauty, and something else repelled, seemed inauthentic, made him fear disappointment. It was the old, learned, and long-nourished timidity in the face of what he felt to be sluttish, a fear of conscious display of beauty, of frank reminders of sex and sexual combat. He felt quite clearly that the dichotomy lay within himself. Here was Wagner again, here again was the world of beauty, but without decency, of charm but without concealment, without *pudeur*, without guilty conscience. There was an enemy within him who barred the way to paradise.

The tables were now being moved by the waiters so that there was a clear area in the centre. Some of the guests had not returned.

'Stay,' one impulse bade the lonely man. He could foresee the kind of night awaiting him if he left now. A night like the last, probably even worse. Little sleep, evil dreams, hopelessness and self-torment, along with the wail of the senses, the thought of that string of green stones on the woman's white and pearly breast. Perhaps soon, very soon, he would reach the point at which life could no longer be endured. And strangely enough he was nevertheless attached to life. Or was he? But would he be here otherwise? Would he have left his wife, burned his boats behind him; would he have set this whole terrible course of things going, made all these incisions into his own flesh, if he were not attached to life, if there were not longings and a sense of the future within him? Had he not felt the goodness of life today, so clearly and beautifully, over the good wine, at the closed park gate, on the bench at the lakeside?

He stayed and found a seat at the table beside the one where the singer and the yellow-haired girl sat. There were six or seven persons sitting around it, obviously at home here, in a sense part of the place and the entertainment. He fixed his eyes upon them. They seemed on intimate terms with some of the patrons of this garden restaurant. The members of the orchestra also knew them and went to their table or called out jokes to them now and then. They addressed the waiters by their first names. German, Italian, and French were being spoken all at once in gay confusion.

Klein studied the yellow-haired girl. She remained cool and grave; he had not yet seen her smiling. Her controlled face seemed impassive. He could see that she counted for something at her table; the men and girls took a tone of comradely respect towards her. He also heard her name said: Teresina. Was she beautiful, he considered; did he really like her? He could not say. Undoubtedly her figure and her walk were beautiful, unusually so in fact, as was her posture while sitting and the movements of her very well groomed hands. But the quiet coolness of her face irritated him, the composure of its expression, the almost masklike immobility. She looked like a person who has his own heaven and his own hell, which no one can share with him. This was a person with a hard, brittle, perhaps proud and even spiteful spirit; yet in her too desires and passions must burn. What kinds of feelings did she love and seek, what kinds did she flee? Where were her weaknesses, her anxieties, her concealments? How did she look when she laughed, when she slept, when she wept, when she kissed?

And how was it that she had been occupying his thoughts for half a day now, that he was watching her, studying her, fearing her, angered by her, when he did not even know yet whether or not he liked her?

Was she possibly a destination for him, part of his destiny? Was some secret power attracting him to her, as a power had drawn him to the south? An innate impulse, a line of fate, a lifelong unconscious urge? Perhaps their meeting was predestined. Imposed upon him.

By listening strenuously he managed to pick a fragment of her conversation out of the general chatter. To a dapper young man with wavy black hair and a smooth face he heard her saying: 'Some time I'd like to really gamble again, not here, not for chocolates, but over in Castiglione or in Monte Carlo.' And then, in reply to whatever he'd said, she continued: 'No, you can't realize what it's like. Perhaps it's ugly, perhaps it's irrational, but it's intoxicating.'

Now he knew something about her. It gave him great pleasure to have eavesdropped on her. Through a small illuminated window he, the stranger, standing at his post outside, had been able to cast a brief spy's look into her heart. She had desires. She craved something exciting and dangerous, something at which you could lose. He was pleased to know that. And what was this about Castiglione? Hadn't he heard the name mentioned once before today? Where? When?

No matter, he could not remember just now. But once more he had the feeling, as he had frequently had it during these strange days, that everything he did, heard, saw, and thought was full of allusions and necessity, that a guide was leading him, that long, remote chains of causation were producing their results. Well, let them. That was just as well.

Once again a sense of happiness passed over him, a sense of calm and security, balm for one who had been experiencing anxiety and horror. He recalled a phrase from his boyhood. He and a group of his schoolmates had been talking about how tightrope dancers managed to walk so assuredly and fearlessly on their ropes. And one boy had said: 'If you draw a chalk line on the kitchen floor, it's just as hard to walk right on this chalk line as on the thinnest rope. And yet you do it calmly because there's no danger. If you imagine that it's just a chalk line and the air next to you is a floor, you can walk safely on any rope.' He recalled that now. How fine it was! Perhaps the trouble with him was that he took the reverse view. Perhaps he could no longer walk calmly and safely on a level floor because he mistook it for a rope.

He rejoiced that such consoling ideas could occur to him, that they slumbered within him and came to light every so often. You carried everything that mattered inside yourself; nobody could help you from outside. Not to be at war with yourself, to live with yourself in affection and trust – that was the thing. Then you could do anything. Then you could not only walk a tightrope but fly.

For a while, forgetting everything around him, he yielded to these feelings, groping his way along soft, slippery paths of the psyche like a hunter and scout, sitting absorbed at his table, head propped on his hand. At that moment the yellow-haired girl looked across at him. Her eyes did not linger but read his face attentively, and when he felt her gaze and looked up he sensed something like respect, sympathy, and a touch of kinship. This time her look did not hurt him, did not do him an injustice. This time, he felt, she was looking at him, at his self, not at his clothes and manners, his hair and hands, but at what was true, immutable, and mysterious about him, his individuality, his share in the divine, his fate.

He apologized inwardly for the bitter and hateful things he had thought about her. But no, there was nothing to apologize for. Whatever malice and foolishness he had thought or felt about her, it had all been so many blows directed against himself, not against her. No, all was well.

Suddenly the resumption of the music startled him. The orchestra struck up a dance. But the stage remained empty and dark; the eyes of the patrons turned instead upon the empty rectangle among the tables. He guessed that there would be dancing now.

Looking up, he saw the yellow-haired girl and the smooth-shaven young gallant rising. He smiled at himself as he noticed his hostile

feelings towards this young man also, how unwittingly he acknowledged
his elegance, his good manners, his handsome face and hair. The young
man offered her his hand, led her into the open space. Another couple
stepped forward, and the two couples danced a tango, elegantly, sure-
footedly, and prettily. Klein did not know much about the steps, but he
quickly saw that Teresina danced wonderfully. He saw that she was
doing something she understood and had mastered, something that
came easily to her. The young man with the wavy black hair also danced
well. They suited each other. Their dancing spoke to the spectators of
pleasant, bright, simple, and amiable things. Lightly and delicately,
their hands held one another; gladly and willingly their knees, their
arms, their feet, and their bodies performed their supple work. Their
dance expressed joy and happiness, beauty and luxury, good breeding
and good style. It also expressed love and sexuality, but nothing wild
and passionate, rather a love full of naturalness, *naïveté*, and grace. For
the wealthy patrons of this resort, they danced the beauty which life
held but which these people did not themselves express and could not
even feel without such outside aid. These professional dancers served
as surrogates for high society. Those others, who themselves did not
dance so well and lithely, who could not really enjoy the pleasant
dalliance of their lives, were reminded of nature and the innocence of
feelings and the senses. Out of their rushed and overworked or lazy and
oversatiated lives, which alternated between wild bouts of work, wild
bouts of pleasure, and forced sanatorium penances, they looked on,
smiling, stupid, and secretly touched, at this dance of pretty and agile
young people. For them it was like gazing at the bright springtime of
life, at a distant paradise that they had lost and could tell the children
about only on holidays, scarcely believing in it themselves any longer,
but dreaming of it at night with burning desire.

And now, during the dance, there came over the girl's face a change
that Friedrich Klein watched with pure ecstasy. Very gradually and as
imperceptibly as the flush of pink in a morning sky, a slowly growing,
slowly warming smile spread over her cool, grave face. Looking straight
ahead, she smiled as if awakening, as if only this dance could warm her
coolness and rouse her to full life. The male dancer likewise smiled,
and the second couple also. It was lovely to see a smile awaken on all
four faces, for all of them seemed masklike and impersonal. But on
Teresina's face the smile was the most beautiful and mysterious of all.
None of the others smiled as she did, so untouched by everything outside, as if she were blossoming with pleasure from within. Klein saw

this with deep emotion; it gripped him like the discovery of a hidden treasure.

'What wonderful hair she has,' he heard someone nearby exclaiming softly. He recalled that in his thoughts he had slandered this wonderful blonde hair and doubted its genuineness.

The tango was over. Klein saw Teresina standing beside her partner for a moment. He was still holding her left hand with its slender fingers at shoulder height. The enchantment in her face glowed for a moment longer and slowly vanished. There was applause, and everyone looked at the pair as they returned to their table with springy steps.

The next dance, which began after a brief interlude, was performed only by Teresina and her handsome partner. It was a freely imaginative dance, a small, complicated creation, almost a pantomime, which each dancer played for himself alone and which became a dance for the couple only at a few brilliant climaxes and during the tempestuous final movement.

Teresina floated, her eyes filled with happiness, so utterly relaxed and so blissfully, weightlessly following the cajoling music that everyone watched her raptly. The dance ended in a vigorous whirling during which the partners only touched with their hands and the tips of their feet and then, leaning far over backwards, turned in a bacchic circle.

During this dance everyone had the feeling that the two dancers, in their gestures and steps, in their partings and rejoinings, in their repeated discarding and regaining of equilibrium, were representing feelings that were familiar to all people and deeply desired but that are experienced so simply, so strongly and clearly only by a very few happy souls. Their dance bespoke the joy of a healthy person in himself, the intensification of this joy into love for another, belief in and acceptance of one's own nature, trustful yielding to the wishes, dreams, and games of the heart. For a moment many of the onlookers felt a pensive sadness that there was so much stress and strife in their daily activities, that their lives were not a dance but a toilsome, panting staggering along under heavy burdens – burdens which, after all, only they themselves had loaded on their own shoulders.

While he watched the dance Friedrich Klein sighted down the past years of his life as down a dark tunnel. On the far side, green and shining in sunlight and wind, lay what he had lost: youth, strong, simple feelings, readiness for happiness and belief in its possibility – and all this was once again strangely near, only a step away, brought here by magic and reflected.

The tender smile of the dance still on her face, Teresina now passed by him. Gladness and a rapturous devotion streamed through him. And as if he had summoned her, she suddenly looked tenderly at him, not yet awakened, her spirit still filled with happiness, the sweet smile still on her lips. And he too smiled at her, this nearby gleam of happiness down the dark shaft of so many lost years.

At the same time he stood up and held out his hand to her, like an old friend, without saying a word. Teresina took it and for a moment held it firmly, though she walked on. He followed her. Room was made for him at the artists' table; he now sat beside Teresina and saw the oblong green stones sparkling on the light skin of her throat.

He did not take part in the talk, understanding very little of it. Behind Teresina's head he saw, in the light of the garden lanterns, the blooming rose bushes as full dark spheres, over which fireflies occasionally flew. His thoughts rested; there was nothing to think about. The spheres of roses swayed lightly in the night breeze. Teresina sat beside him, the green gem glittering on her ear. The world was in order.

Now Teresina placed her hand on his arm.

'We will talk. Not here. I remember seeing you in the park. I'll be there tomorrow at the same time. I am tired now and have to get my full night's sleep. You'd better go first, otherwise my friends will be borrowing money from you.'

As a waiter went past, she stopped him.

'Eugenio, the gentleman wants his check.'

He paid, shook hands with her, tipped his hat, and left, walking towards the lake, not knowing where he was going. Impossible to lie down in his hotel room now. He walked on the path by the lake, away from the town and suburbs, until the parks and benches along the shore came to an end. Then he sat down on the wall of the embankment and sang under his breath, voicelessly, half-forgotten fragments of songs from the years of his young manhood. He stayed until it turned cold and the steep mountains took on a hostile, alien air. Then he walked back, holding his hat in his hand.

A sleepy night clerk opened the door for him.

'Yes, I'm rather late,' Klein said, giving him a franc.

'Oh, we're used to that. You aren't the last to come in. The motorboat from Castiglione isn't back yet either.'

Chapter Three

The dancer was already there when Klein entered the park. She was walking with her buoyant step around a sector of lawn, and suddenly stood facing him at the shady entrance to a copse.

Teresina's light-grey eyes probed him attentively. Her expression was earnest and somewhat impatient. While walking, she began to talk.

'Can you tell me what happened yesterday? How is it we kept running across each other? I've been thinking about that. I saw you yesterday in the garden twice. The first time you were standing at the exit looking at me. You looked bored or irritated, and as soon as I saw you I remembered that I'd already run across you in the park. I didn't have a good impression, and I made an effort to forget you right away. Then I saw you again, barely fifteen minutes later. You were sitting at the next table and suddenly looked entirely different, and I didn't realize right away that you were the same man I'd met before. And then, after my dance, you suddenly stood up and took my hand, or I took yours, I'm not sure which. What was going on? You must know something, you really must. But I hope you haven't come here to make me declarations of love.'

'I don't know,' Klein said. 'I haven't come with anything definite in mind. I love you, since yesterday, but we needn't talk about that, you know.'

'Yes, let's talk about something else. Yesterday there was something between us for a moment that bothers me and also frightens me, as though we had some similarity or something in common. What is it?

And the main thing I wanted to ask: What was that strange change in you? How was it possible that within an hour you could have two such entirely different faces? You looked like a person who has experienced something very important.'

'How did I look?' he asked childishly.

'Oh, at first you looked like a rather grumpy, disagreeable middle-aged gentleman. You looked like a philistine, like a man who is used to taking out on others his anger over his own insufficiencies.'

He listened with eager sympathy, nodding vigorously. She continued:

'And then, afterwards, it's hard to describe. You were sitting some-what stooped. When I happened to notice you, my first thought was: Good Lord, what sad postures these philistines have. You were holding your head propped in your hand, and suddenly that looked so odd. It looked as if you were the only person in the world, and as if you didn't care one bit what happened to you or to the whole world. Your face was like a mask, horribly sad or maybe horribly indifferent . . .'

She broke off and seemed to be groping for words, but then said nothing further.

'You are right,' Klein said meekly. 'You saw so accurately that I can't help being amazed. You read me like a letter. But of course I suppose it is only natural and right that you should be able to see all that.'

'Why so?'

'Because in a different way, while dancing, you express the same thing. When you dance, Teresina, and at many other moments too, you're like a tree or a mountain or an animal, or like a star, altogether alone, altogether by yourself. You don't want to be anything different from what you are, whether good or bad. Isn't that the same thing you saw in me?'

She studied him without replying. Then she said falteringly: 'You are a strange person. And what about now: are you still that way? Do you not care at all what happens to you?'

'Yes. Only not always. I'm often frightened, too. But then it comes again and the fear is gone and then nothing matters. Then I feel strong. Or rather, it's not quite right to say I feel that nothing matters; every-thing is precious and welcome, no matter what it is.'

'For a moment I even thought you might be a criminal.'

'That is possible too. It's even probable. You see, people say "criminal", and by this they mean that someone does something that others have forbidden him to do. But he himself, the criminal, only does what is in him. You see, there is the resemblance between us; both of us here and now, at rare moments, do what is in us. Nothing is rarer. Most people can't do that at all. I used not to be able to, either. I said, thought, acted, lived only what came from others, only things I'd learned, only good and proper things, until one day that was all over. I couldn't keep it up, I had to leave; the good things weren't good any longer and the proper things no longer proper. Life was no longer bearable. But still I want to bear it. I even love it, although it brings with it so many torments.'

'Will you tell me your name and who you are?'

'I'm the man you see before you, that is all. I have no name and no title and no occupation either. I've had to give all that up. It's this way: after a long, decent, hard-working life I fell out of the nest one day. It wasn't long ago. And now I must die or learn to fly. The world no longer concerns me; I'm all alone now.'

Rather embarrassed, she asked: 'Were you in an institution?'

'You mean insane? No. Although that too would be possible.' He was distracted; thoughts welling up from within seized hold of him. With the beginnings of uneasiness he continued: 'When we talk about such things, the simplest matters immediately become complicated and incomprehensible. We should not talk about them at all. People only do that, talk about such things, when they don't want to understand one another.'

'How do you mean that? I really want to understand. Believe me, I do. It interests me tremendously.'

He gave a lively smile.

'Yes, yes. You want to entertain yourself with this subject. You have experienced something and now want to talk about it. But it's no use. Talking is the surest way to misunderstand everything, to make everything shallow and dreary. You don't want to understand me, or yourself either. You want only to be left alone, not to be troubled by the warning you've received. You want to dismiss me and the warning by finding the label you can fit to me. You've tried it with the idea of a criminal and a madman. You want to know my name and status. But all that only leads away from understanding. It's all a deception, my dear young lady; it's a bad substitute for understanding; it's an escape from wanting to understand, from being forced to understand.'

He broke off and tormentedly brushed his hand over his eyes. Then something pleasanter seemed to occur to him. He smiled again: 'You know, yesterday when for a moment you and I felt exactly the same thing, we said nothing and asked no questions, did not even think anything either; suddenly we took each other's hands and all was well. But now – now we are talking and thinking and explaining and everything has become odd and incomprehensible, everything that was so simple before. And yet it would be very easy for you to understand me just as well as I understand you.'

'Do you think you understand me so well?'

'Yes, of course. I don't know how you live. But you live as I too have done and as everybody does, mostly in darkness and self-oblivion, pursuing some purpose, some duty, some plan. Almost everybody does that; the whole world is sick of doing it and is doomed because of it. But sometimes, when dancing, for example, you lose touch with your plan or duty and suddenly you find yourself living another way entirely. You feel all at once as if you were alone in the world, or as if you might be dead tomorrow, and then everything you really are comes out. When you dance, you even infect others with that feeling. That is your secret.'

They walked on more quickly for a while. Where a spit of land thrust into the lake, they stood still.

'You are strange,' she said. 'I can understand some of the things you say. But – what do you really want of me?'

He bowed his head and for a moment looked sad.

'You are used to having people always want something of you, Teresina. I don't want anything of you that you yourself don't want and would not gladly do. That I love you need not matter to you. It is no happiness to be loved. Everyone loves himself, yet thousands of people torment themselves all their lives. No, to be loved is not happiness. But loving – that is happiness!'

'I would gladly do something that gives you pleasure, if I could,' Teresina said slowly, as if pitying him.

'You can do that if you allow me to fulfil some wish of yours.'

'Oh, what do you know about my wishes!'

'I grant you, you shouldn't have any. For you have the key to paradise – your dancing. But I know you do have wishes nevertheless, and I am glad of that. And so you ought to know this: here is someone who will take pleasure in fulfilling your every wish.'

Teresina considered. Her alert eyes turned sharp and cool again. What could he possibly know about her? Since she could not think what this might be, she began cautiously. 'The first thing I'd like to ask you is to be honest. Tell me who has told you anything about me.'

'No one. I have never spoken with a soul about you. What I know – it is very little – I have learned from you yourself. I heard you say yester-day that you wish you could gamble in Castiglione once.'

Her face twitched. 'Oh, I see. You were eavesdropping on me.'

'Yes, of course. I understood your wish. Because you are not always at one with yourself, you seek excitement and distraction.'

'Oh no, I'm not as romantic as you think. I'm not looking for dis-traction in gambling, but just for money. I'd like to be rich some day, or at any rate free of cares, without having to sell myself for it. That's all.'

'That sounds so right, and yet I don't believe it. But as you like. At bottom you know perfectly well that you need never sell yourself. Let's not talk about it. But if you want money, whether for gambling or any-thing else, please take it from me. I have more than I need, and believe me, I place no value on it.'

Teresina drew away from him. 'I hardly know you. How can I take money from you?'

He suddenly pulled his hat off, as if attacked by a pain, and did not answer.

'What's the matter?' Teresina exclaimed.

'Nothing, nothing. Permit me to leave now. We've talked too much, much too much. People should never talk so much.'

He was already walking off, without saying goodbye, speeding down the lane of trees as if blown by despair. Teresina looked after him with choked-up, divided feelings, astonished at him and at herself.

He was not running away out of despair but out of unbearable tension and charged emotions. It had suddenly become impossible for him to say another word, to hear another word; he had to be alone, could not be other than alone, thinking, listening to himself, probing himself. The whole conversation with Teresina had thrown him into a state of amaze-ment at himself. The words had come without his willing them; he had been overcome by a violent need to communicate his experiences and thoughts, to form them, say them, tell them to himself. He was aston-ished at every word he had heard himself saying; but more and more he could feel that he had been talking himself into something that was no longer simple and right, that he had been uselessly trying to explain the inexplicable. And suddenly the whole thing had become unbearable to him, so that he had to stop it.

But now, when he tried to recall these past fifteen minutes, he grate-fully felt the experience to have been a joyful one. It was progress, a step towards release, a confirmation.

The doubts he had been feeling about his whole customary world had tormented him and terribly wearied him. He had experienced the miracle that life becomes more meaningful precisely when we lose our grasp of all meanings. But again and again had come the painful doubt whether these experiences were really significant, whether they were no more than minor ripples on the surface of his fatigued and sick mind, basically whims, petty nervous stirrings. Now, last night and today, he had seen that his experience was real. It had radiated out of him and changed him, had drawn another person to him. His solitude was shattered; he was in love again; there was someone whom he could serve, someone to whom he wanted to give pleasure. He could smile again, laugh again.

The wave passed through him like pain and like voluptuous delight. He trembled with sheer emotion. Life roared in him like surf. Everything was incomprehensible. He opened his eyes wide and saw: trees on a street, slivers of silver in the lake, a running dog, bicyclists – and everything was strange, like a fairy tale, and almost too beautiful. Everything looked as if it had come brand-new out of God's toy box. Everything existed for him alone, for Friedrich Klein, and he himself existed solely to feel this stream of wonder and pain and joy pouring through himself. There was beauty everywhere, in every rubbish heap by the wayside; there was deep suffering everywhere; God was everything. Yes, all this was God, and in the unimaginably distant past, as a boy, he had once felt Him that way, and had sought Him with his heart whenever he thought 'God' and 'Almighty.' Let not my heart break with overflowing.

Once more, from all the forgotten shafts of his life, released memories rushed forth. They came without number: conversations, the period of his engagement, clothes he had worn as a child, vacation mornings during his student days. The memories arranged themselves in circles around certain fixed points: the image of his wife, his mother, Wagner the murderer, Teresina. Passages from classical writers occurred to him, and Latin proverbs that had once moved him in his schooldays, and foolish, sentimental lines from folk songs. The shadow of his father stood behind him. Once again he lived through the time of his mother-in-law's death. Everything that had ever passed into him through eyes or ears, through people or books, all the delight and the anguish that had been buried within him, seemed to be present again, all at the same time, all stirred together and whirling chaotically but meaningfully. It was all there, all significant; nothing had been lost.

The pressure became a torture that could not be distinguished from

extreme voluptuous pleasure. His heart beat rapidly. Tears filled his
eyes. He realized that he was on the verge of madness and yet knew that
he would not go mad, while at the same time he was peering into this
new psychic landscape of madness with the same astonishment and
rapture as into the past, as into the lake or the sky. There too everything
was enchanted, mellifluous and full of meaning. He understood why
madness, in the minds of great-hearted peoples, was considered sacred.
He understood everything; everything spoke to him, everything was
revealed to him. There were no words for this state. It was wrong and
hopeless to cogitate about it and try to apprehend it in words. The thing
was to be receptive, to hold yourself in readiness; then all things, the
whole world, could enter into you in an infinite parade as if you were a
kind of Noah's Ark. And then you possessed the world, understood it,
were one with it.

Sadness swept him. If only all men knew this, could experience this!
How carelessly people lived, carelessly sinned; how blindly and im-
moderately people suffered. Had he not been annoyed with Teresina
only yesterday? Had he not, only yesterday, hated his wife, hurled
accusations against her and tried to blame her for all the suffering in his
life? How sad, how stupid, how hopeless. Why, everything was so
simple, so good, so meaningful, as soon as you saw things from inside,
as soon as you saw the essence dwelling behind everything, saw Him,
God.

Here a road forked off to new gardens of the imagination, new forests
of imagery. If he turned his present feeling towards the future, a
hundred realms of happiness rose up like fireworks and spread open for
him and for everyone. There was no need to lament, to accuse, to judge
his apathetic, ruined life. Rather, it could be transformed into its opposite, could be seen as full of meaning, full of joy, full of kindliness, full
of love. The grace he had just experienced must be radiated out and
affect others. Phrases from the Bible came into his mind, and everything
he knew about the blessed and the saints. This was how it had always
begun, for all of them. They had been led the same harsh and gloomy
way as himself, had been cowardly and full of fears until the hour of
conversion and illumination. 'In the world ye have fear,' Jesus had said
to his disciples. But one who had overcome fear no longer lived in the
world, but in God, in eternity.

They had all taught this, all the sages of the entire world, Buddha and
Schopenhauer, Jesus, the Greeks. There was only one wisdom, only one
faith, only one philosophy: the knowledge that God is within us. How

that was twisted and mistaught in schools, churches, books, and scholarly disciplines!

Klein's mind flew through the realms of his inner world, his knowledge, his education. Here too, as in his outward life, treasure upon treasure was stored, wellspring upon wellspring; but each was by itself, isolated, dead and worthless. Now, however, struck by the ray of illumination, order, meaning, and shape suddenly appeared in the chaos, creation began, life and relevance leaped from pole to pole. The statements of abstruse contemplation became obvious, obscurities appeared bright, and the multiplication table was transformed into a mystical experience. This world, too, acquired animation and glowed with love. The works of art that he had loved in his younger years reverberated in his mind with fresh enchantment. He saw now that the same key opened the mysterious sphere of art. Art was nothing but regarding the world in a state of grace: illumination. Art was revealing God behind all things.

Afire with this new blessing, he strode through the world. Every twig on every tree shared in an ecstasy, pointed upward more nobly, hung downward more delicately, was symbol and revelation. Violet shadows of clouds played over the surface of the lake, quivering with frail sweetness. Every stone lay significantly beside its shadow. Never had the world been so beautiful, so deeply and sacredly lovable, or at least never since the mysterious, legendary years of early childhood. 'Unless you become as little children . . .' occurred to him, and he felt: I have become a child again, I have entered into the Kingdom of Heaven.

When he began to be conscious of fatigue and hunger, he found himself far from the city. Now he remembered where he had come from, what had happened, and that he had run away from Teresina without a word of parting. In the next village, he looked for a restaurant. A small rural tavern with a wooden table in a tiny garden, beneath a cherry laurel, attracted him. He asked for a meal, but they had nothing but wine and bread. How about soup, he asked, or eggs, or ham. No, they did not have such things here. People here were not ordering anything of the sort in these dear times. He had talked first with the woman who ran the tavern, then with a grandmother who was sitting on the stone threshold at the door of the house, mending linen. Now he sat down in the garden, under the deep shade of the tree, with bread and tart red wine. In the adjoining garden, invisible behind a grape arbour and washing on the line, he heard two girls singing. Suddenly a word of the song stabbed his heart, without his grasping what it was. It was repeated

in the next verse; it was the name Teresina. The song, a partly comic
one, dealt with a girl named Teresina. He made out:

> *La sua mamma alla finestra*
> *Con una voce serpentina:*
> *Vieni a casa, o Teresina,*
> *Lasc' andare quel traditor!*

Teresina! How he loved her. How glorious it was to love.

He laid his head on the table and dozed, fell asleep and awakened
again, several times. It was evening. The woman who ran the tavern
came and planted herself in front of the table, perplexed by this patron.
He placed money on the table, asked for another glass of wine, and
queried her about the song. She became friendly, brought the wine, and
stood by. He had her repeat the words of the whole Teresina song, and
was particularly delighted with the stanza:

> *Io non sono traditore*
> *E ne meno lusinghero,*
> *Io son' figlio d'un ricco signore,*
> *Son' venuto per fare l'amor.*

The woman said he could have soup now if he wanted some, she
would be cooking it for her husband anyhow; she was expecting him
home soon.

He ate vegetable soup and bread. The husband came home; the late
sun faded on the grey stone roofs of the village. He asked for a room and
was offered a small chamber with thick, bare stone walls. He took it.
Never before had he slept in such a chamber; it seemed to him like the
den in some story of robbers. Now he strolled through the village, found
a small grocery store still open, bought chocolate and distributed it
among the children who were swarming along the single street. They
ran after him; parents greeted him; everyone wished him a good night,
and he returned the greeting, nodded to all the old and young people
who sat on the thresholds and front steps of the houses.

With pleasure he thought of his chamber in the tavern, that primitive,
cavelike den where the ancient mortar was flaking from the grey walls on
which nothing useless was hung, no pictures, no mirror, no wallpaper or
curtain. He walked through the twilight village as if it were an adventure; everything glowed, everything was filled with secret promise.

Returning to the osteria, where the tiny public room was dark and deserted, he saw a light coming from a crack, followed it, and entered the kitchen. The room seemed like a cavern in a fairy tale. The sparse light flowed over a red tile floor and before it reached the walls and ceiling ebbed away in dense, warm dusk, and from the enormous, intensely black suspended chimney hood an inexhaustible spring of darkness seemed to flow out.

The innkeeper's wife was sitting with the grandmother. The two sat stooped, small, and weak on low, humble stools, their hands resting on their knees. The wife was weeping; both of them ignored Klein as he entered. He sat down on the edge of the table beside remnants of vegetables. A knife gleamed dully; in the glow of light, polished copper pans shone red on the walls. The woman wept; the grey-haired old woman murmured encouragement in the dialect. Gradually Klein understood that there was dissension in the house and that the husband had left again after a quarrel. Klein asked whether the man had struck her, but received no answer. After a while he began to offer consolations. He said the husband would certainly return shortly. The woman said sharply: 'Not today and maybe not tomorrow either.' He gave up. The woman sat up straighter. Her weeping stopped. They sat in silence. The simplicity of it all, the lack of discussion, seemed to him wonderful. There had been a quarrel, she had been hurt, had wept. Now it was over; now she sat still and waited. Life would go on. As with children. As with animals. If only you did not talk, did not make simple things complicated, did not turn your soul inside out.

Klein requested the grandmother to make coffee for all three of them. The women revived; the grandmother promptly put twigs into the fireplace. There was a crackle of breaking wood, of paper, of flame catching. In the sudden flare of the firelight he saw the wife's face, illuminated from beneath, somewhat woebegone but calmer. She looked into the fire, smiling occasionally. Suddenly she stood up, went slowly over to the faucet, and washed her hands.

Then all three of them sat at the kitchen table drinking the hot black coffee and an aged juniper liqueur. The women became livelier, told stories and asked questions, laughed at Klein's painful and incorrect Italian. It seemed to him he had been here for a long, long time. Strange, how much room there was for so many things these days. Whole eras and periods of life fitted into an afternoon; every hour seemed overladen with the cargo of life. For brief seconds a fear flashed within him like sheet lightning that fatigue and consumption of his vitality might assail him with hundredfold intensity and burn him away like the sun licking a drop of water from a rock. In those fleeting but recurrent moments of alien lightning he saw himself living, felt and saw inside his brain, and observed there the quickened oscillations of an inexpressibly complicated, delicate, and precious apparatus vibrating with multiple tasks, like a highly sensitive watchworks shielded behind glass because a grain of dust suffices to disturb it.

He learned that the innkeeper put his money into uncertain ventures, stayed away from home a great deal, and had affairs with women. The couple had no children. While Klein made efforts to find the Italian words for simple questions, the delicate watchworks clicked restlessly away behind glass, in a subtle fever, instantly including every lived moment in its calculations and considerations.

Before the night wore on too long, he stood up to go to bed. He shook hands with both women, and the young wife looked probingly at him while the grandmother fought not to yawn. Then he groped his way up the dark staircase, finding the steps astonishingly high, to his room. There he found water in a pitcher, washed his face, for a moment felt the lack of soap, slippers, and nightshirt. He spent another quarter hour at the window, leaning on the granite sill, then undressed completely and lay down in the hard bed. The coarse sheets delighted him and brought a flood of pleasant rustic images. Was this not the only right thing, to live in a room consisting of four stone walls, without the ridiculous paraphernalia of wallpapers, ornaments, furniture, without all those exaggerated and basically barbarian incidentals? A roof overhead against the rain, a simple blanket over you against the cold, bread and wine or milk against hunger, the sun to wake you in the morning, the darkness to lull you to sleep at evening – did a man need more?

But as soon as he had put out the light, the house and the room and the village vanished. He was standing by the lake with Teresina again and talking with her. He had difficulty remembering today's conversation and was doubtful about what he had actually said to her, even wondered whether the whole meeting had not been a dream, an illusion of his. The darkness felt good – God only knew where he would wake in the morning.

A noise at the door waked him. Softly, the latch was moved; a thread of light entered and hesitated in the crack. Startled and yet at the moment understanding, he looked towards it, not yet fully in the present. Then the door opened; barefoot, a candle in her hand, the innkeeper's wife stood there, silent. She looked searchingly over at him, and he smiled and held out his arms, without thought. Then she was beside him and her dark hair lay beside his face on the rough pillow.

They did not say a word. Inflamed by her kiss, he drew her to him. The sudden nearness and human warmth against his chest, the strong, unfamiliar arm around his neck, moved him strangely – how alien, how unknown, how painfully new this warmth and closeness was for him – how alone he had been, how terribly alone, how long alone! Abysses and infernos had gaped between himself and all the rest of the world, and now a stranger had come to him, in wordless trust and in need of comfort, a poor, neglected woman just as he had for years been a neglected and intimidated man, and she clung to his neck and gave and took and greedily sucked a drop of delight out of the barrenness of life, drunkenly but shyly sought his mouth, let her sadly delicate fingers play in his, rubbed her cheek against his. He raised himself above her pallid face and kissed her on both closed eyes and thought: she thinks she is taking and does not know that she is giving; in her loneliness she has fled to me and does not suspect my loneliness. Only now did he see, for he had been sitting blindly beside her all evening long, that she had long slender hands and fingers, graceful shoulders, and a face full of anxiety over her fate and full of blind hunger for children, and found that she possessed a shy knowledge of little, delicious ways and practices of lovemaking.

He also realized, with sorrow, that he himself had remained a boy and a beginner in love, had become resigned in the course of a long, lukewarm marriage, was timid and yet without innocence, lustful yet full of guilt. Even while he clung with thirsty kisses to the woman's mouth and breast, even while he felt her hand tenderly and almost maternally on his hair, he was already anticipating disappointment and was conscious of a pressure around his heart. He felt the horror of anxiety returning, and with it there flowed through him like icy water the fear and the foreboding that deep within himself he was incapable of love, that love was a kind of evil spell that could bring him only torment. Even before the brief storm of lust had subsided, timidity and suspicion cast an evil eye upon his mind. Already he was disgruntled that he had been taken instead of taking and conquering. The anticipation of disgust came before disgust itself.

Silently, the woman slipped away, taking her candle. Klein lay in the darkness, and in the midst of satiation the moment arrived, that evil moment he had feared hours before during those premonitory flashes of sheet lightning. The excessively ornate music of his new life now found only tired and mistuned strings within him; his feelings of pleasure suddenly had to be paid for with lassitude and dread. With pounding heart, he felt all his enemies lurking in ambush: sleeplessness, depression, and the glimmerings of nightmares. The rough sheets burned against his skin; moonlight glared through the window. Impossible to stay here, helpless before the coming torments. Ah, here it was again, the guilt and the dread were coming again, the sadness and despair. All that he had overcome, the whole of the past, was returning. There was no salvation.

Hastily, he dressed, without light, found his dusty shoes at the door, stole down the stairs and out of the house, and walked swiftly, desperately, on weary, sagging legs, through the village and the night, despising himself, lashing himself, hating himself.

Chapter Four

Struggling, despairing, Klein fought with his demon. All the new understanding and sense of redemption this fateful time had yielded had surged, in the course of this past day, to such a wave of thought and clarity that he had felt he would remain forever on the crest even while he was beginning to drop down. Now he was in the trough again, still fighting, still secretly hoping, but gravely injured. For one brief, glowing day he had succeeded in practising the simple art known to every blade of grass. For one scant day he had loved himself, felt himself to be unified and whole, not split into hostile parts; he had loved himself and the world and God in himself, and everywhere he went he had met nothing but love, approval, and joy. If a robber had attacked him yesterday, or a policeman had arrested him, that too would have been approval, harmony, the smile of fate. And now, in the midst of happiness, he had reversed course and was cutting himself down again. He sat in judgement on himself while his deepest self knew that all judgement was wrong and foolish. The world, which for the span of one day had been crystal clear and wholly filled with divinity, once more presented a harsh and painful face; every object had its own meaning and every meaning contradicted every other. The inspiration of this day had been so perishable. It had been mere whim, and what had happened with Teresina was all imagination, and the adventure in the tavern a dubious and disreputable affair.

He already knew that the choking feeling of dread would pass only if he stopped condemning and admonishing himself, if he stopped poking around in the old wounds. He knew that all pain, all stupidity, all evil became its opposite if he could recognize God in it, if he pursued it to its deepest roots, which extended far beyond weal and woe and good and evil. He knew that. But there was nothing to do about it; the evil spirit was in him, God was a word again, lovely but remote. He hated and despised himself, and this hatred came over him, when the time was ripe, as involuntarily and inexorably as love and trustfulness at other times. And this was how it always must be. Again and again and again he would experience the grace and blessing, and again and again the accursed contrary. His life would never follow the path that his own will prescribed for him. A plaything and a floating cork, he would eternally be bandied back and forth. Until the end came, until sooner or later a wave broke over him, and death or madness received him. If only that might be soon!

Compulsively, the bitterly familiar thoughts returned, useless cares, useless anxieties, useless self-accusations, and realizing their folly was only one more torment. An idea recurred that he had had on his recent journey (months had passed since then, so it seemed): how good it would be to throw himself head first under a train. He pursued the image greedily, inhaling it like ether: head first, everything smashed and ground to splinters, wrapped around the wheels and crushed to powder on the rails. His anguish devoured these visions; with approval and voluptuous pleasure he saw and tasted the complete destruction of Friedrich Klein, felt his heart and brain being rent, splashed, crushed, the aching head bashed open, the aching eyes squeezed out, the liver flattened, the kidneys smashed, the hair torn away, the bones, knees, and chin pulverized. That was what the killer Wagner had wanted to feel when he drowned his wife, his children, and himself in blood. That was it exactly. Oh, he understood him so well. He himself was Wagner, a man of excellent qualities, capable of sensing divinity, capable of loving, but much too burdened, much too reflective, much too easily fatigued, much too well versed in his defects and afflictions. What in the world should such a man, such a Wagner, such a Klein, do? Forever seeing before his eyes that chasm separating him from God, forever feeling the crack in the world running through his own heart, exhausted, worn out by that eternal soaring towards God that everlastingly ended in falling back – what else should such a Wagner, such a Klein do but extinguish himself, himself and everything that could possibly be a reminder of him, cast himself back into the dark womb out of which the Inconceivable for ever and ever expelled the transitory world of forms? No, nothing else was possible! Wagner must go, Wagner must die, Wagner must erase himself from the book of life. It might be useless to kill yourself, might be ridiculous. Perhaps everything respectable people in that world he had left said about suicide was altogether right. But was there anything at all for a man in this state which would not be useless, not be ridiculous? No, nothing. Far better to have your head under the wheels of a train, to feel the skull crack, to plunge deliberately into the abyss.

His knees repeatedly giving way, he kept moving on hour after hour. He lay for a while on railroad tracks that crossed the road, actually dozed off with his head on the steel rail, awoke again and had forgotten what he wanted, stood up and reeled on, the soles of his feet aching, shooting pains in his head, sometimes falling, scratched by thorns, sometimes floating lightly along, sometimes forcing every step with great effort.

'Now the devil ripely rides me!' he sang hoarsely under his breath. Ah, to ripen! To be grilled brown, painfully, to be roasted completely, like the pit in a peach, to be ripe, to be able to die!

There was a spark floating in this darkness. He clung to it with all the ardour of his racked soul. It was a thought: useless to kill himself, to kill himself now; no point to exterminating himself, tearing himself limb from limb – it was useless. But it was good and redeeming to suffer, to ferment to ripeness amid tears and tortures, to be forged to completion amid blows and pangs. Then you had earned the right to die, and then dying was good, beautiful, and meaningful, the greatest blessing in the world, more blissful than any night of love: burned out and utterly resigned to fall back into the womb, to be extinguished, redeemed, reborn. Such a death, such a ripe and good, noble death, alone had meaning; it alone was salvation, it alone was homecoming. Longing cried in his heart. Where, where was the narrow, difficult path, where was the gateway? He was ready; with every quiver of his exhausted, agitated body, of his anguished mind, he yearned for it.

When the morning greyed in the sky and the leaden lake awoke with its first cool flash of silver, the harried man was standing in a small chestnut grove, high above the lake and the city, among ferns and high, flowering spireas damp with dew. With lifeless eyes, but smiling, he stared down into the strange world. He had reached the goal of his obsessive wanderings; he was so dead tired that his terrified spirit was silent. And above all, the night was over. The battle had been fought, a peril overcome. Felled by exhaustion, he dropped like a dead man among the fern and roots on the ground, his head in a bilberry bush.

The world melted away from his fading senses. His hands clenched among the ferns, his face and chest against the soil, he yielded hungrily to slumber as if it were the longed-for last sleep.

In a dream, of which he could afterwards recall only a few fragments, he saw a door that looked like the entrance to a theatre. On it a large poster with huge lettering read (this was undecided) either *Lohengrin* or 'Wagner'. He entered. Inside was a woman who resembled the inn-keeper's wife, but also his own wife. Her head was distorted; it was too large and the face changed to a horrible mask. He was seized by an over-whelming repugnance for this woman and drove a knife into her abdomen. But another woman, like a mirror image of the first, attacked him from behind, drove sharp, powerful claws into his throat and tried to strangle him.

Waking from this deep sleep, he saw with astonishment the trees above him. He was stiff from lying on the hard ground, but refreshed. With a faint note of dreadfulness, the dream reverberated within him. What strange, naïve, and African games of the imagination! he thought, smiling for a moment as the door with its invitation to enter the 'Wagner' theatre returned to his memory. What an idea, to represent his relationship with Wagner in this way. The spirit of the dream was coarse, but brilliant. It hit the nail on the head. The theatre called 'Wagner' – was that not himself, was it not an invitation to enter into his own interior being, into the foreign land of his true self? For Wagner was himself – Wagner was the murderer and the hunted man within him, but Wagner was also the composer, the artist, the genius, the seducer, lover of life and the senses, luxury – Wagner was the collective name for everything repressed, buried, scanted in the life of Friedrich Klein, the former civil servant. And *Lohengrin* – was not he himself Lohengrin, the errant knight with the mysterious goal who had to hide his name? The rest was not clear: the woman with the horrible mask of a face and the other woman with the claws. Stabbing her belly with the knife also reminded him of something, and he hoped he would still be able to find what it was – the mood of murder and deadly peril was oddly and harshly mingled with that of theatres, masks, and carni-val.

At the thought of the woman and the knife he distinctly saw, for a moment, his connubial bedroom. Then his mind leaped to the children – how had he been able to forget them! He thought of them clambering out of their little beds in their nightshirts each morning. Their names came into his mind, especially Elly's. Oh, the children! Slowly, tears ran from his eyes down his tired face. He shook his head, rose to his feet with an effort, and began picking leaves and crumbs of soil from his rumpled clothes. Only now did he clearly recall the previous night, the bare stone chamber in the village inn, the woman in his arms, his flight, his driven, endless tramping. He beheld this distorted little fragment of life as a sick man looks at his emaciated hand or the eczema on his leg.

In composed sadness, with tears still brimming in his eyes, he murmured softly to himself: 'God, what do you still have in mind for me?' Of the thoughts of the night, only one yearning voice continued to reverberate within him: the cry for ripeness, for homecoming, for permission to die. Was the way he had to go still far? Was home still remote? Was there much more suffering to come, suffering still inconceivable? He was prepared for it; he offered himself. His heart was open to fate. Strike away!

Walking slowly, he descended through meadows and vineyards towards the city. He went to his hotel, washed and combed himself, changed his clothes. He went to dine, drank some of the good wine, and felt the weariness in his stiff limbs diminishing and giving way to pleasurable feelings. He asked when the dancing began in the Rose Garden, and went there at teatime.

Teresina was dancing when he entered. He saw that curiously glowing dance-smile on her face again, and rejoiced. He greeted her when she returned to her table, and went to speak to her.

'I'd like to ask you to come to Castiglione with me this evening,' he said softly.

She considered.

'Today, right off?' she asked. 'Is there such a hurry?'

'I can wait if you prefer. But it would be nice. Where shall we meet?'

She did not resist the invitation, or the childlike smile that for seconds clung to his furrowed, lonely face, making it oddly handsome, like a brave wallpaper on the last wall of a burned and collapsed house.

'Where have you been?' she asked curiously. 'You disappeared so suddenly yesterday. And every time I see you, you have a different face. Again today. You aren't a drug addict, by any chance?'

He only laughed, with an oddly handsome and rather alien laugh, his mouth and chin looking utterly boyish, while the circlet of thorns remained above his forehead and eyes.

'Call for me at the restaurant of the Hotel Esplanade. I think there is a boat leaving at nine. But tell me what you did yesterday.'

'I think I went walking, most of the day and most of the night. I had to comfort a village woman whose husband had run off. And then I took great pains to learn an Italian song because it dealt with a Teresina.'

'What song is that?'

'It begins: *Su in cima di quel boschetto.*'

'Good heavens, you already know that wretched thing. Yes, it's all the rage among shopgirls now.'

'Oh, I think it's a very pretty song.'

'And you comforted a woman?'

'Yes, she was feeling bad and her husband had run off and was unfaithful to her.'

'I see. And what did you do to make her feel better?'

'She came to me so as not to be alone any longer. I kissed her and lay with her.'

'Was she nice-looking?'

'I don't know, I didn't look close. No, don't laugh, not at that. It was so sad.'

She laughed anyhow. 'How funny you are. Well, and so you didn't sleep at all. You look it.'

'Oh yes, I slept for several hours. In woods, up on the mountain.'

She followed the direction of his finger, which was pointing at the ceiling, and laughed loudly.

'In an inn?'

'No, in the woods. Among the bilberries. They're good, almost ripe.'

'You're a dreamer. But I must dance – the conductor is already tapping. Where are you, Claudio?'

The handsome, dark-haired dancer was standing behind her chair. The music began. At the end of the dance, Klein left.

He called for her punctually that evening and was glad he had worn evening clothes, for Teresina was dressed very festively, in violet, with a great deal of lace; she looked like a princess.

At the beach he led Teresina not to the hotel ferry but to a pretty motorboat he had rented for the evening. They entered; in the half-enclosed cabin, blankets for Teresina lay ready, and flowers. In a tight curve the swift boat shot out of the harbour into the lake.

On the water, surrounded by night and silence, Klein said: 'Teresina, isn't it a pity to go over there now among so many people? If you care to, we can ride on, without a destination, as long as we please, or stop at some quiet, lovely village, drink a country wine and listen to the girls sing. What do you think?'

She did not reply, and he at once saw the disappointment on her face. He laughed.

'No, it was just a notion of mine, forgive me. I want you to be amused and to do what gives you pleasure; that is our only programme. We'll be across in ten minutes.'

'Doesn't the gambling interest you at all?' she asked.

'I'll have to see; I'll have to try it first. At the moment I don't quite see the point of it. Either one wins money or one loses money. I think there are stronger sensations.'

'The money you play for isn't just money. It's more or less a symbol. Everyone wins or loses not just money but all the wishes and dreams that money means to him. If I have money nobody can order me around any more. I'll live the way I like. I'll dance whenever and wherever and for anyone I like. I'll travel wherever I want.'

He interrupted her. 'What a child you are, my dear young lady. There is no such freedom, except in your wishes. If you should become rich and free and independent tomorrow – the day after tomorrow you'll fall in love with some man who'll take the money for himself or cut your throat one night.'

'Don't say such horrible things! All right, if I were rich maybe I would live even more simply than I do now, but I'd do it because it pleased me, voluntarily and not because I have to. I hate having no choice. And you see, if I go ahead and risk my money at the gaming table, all my wishes take part every time I win or lose. I'm staking everything valuable and desirable to me, and that gives you a feeling that's pretty rare.'

Klein watched her as she spoke, without paying close attention to her words. Unwittingly, he compared Teresina's face with the face of the woman he had dreamed of in the woods.

He did not become aware of this until the boat glided into the bay of Castiglione, for there the sight of the illuminated sheet-metal sign with the name of the town violently reminded him of the sign in the dream which had borne the word Lohengrin or Wagner. That was exactly how the sign had looked, just as large, just as grey and white, just as glaringly illuminated. Was this the stage on which he must set foot? Was he coming to Wagner here? Now, too, he became aware that Teresina resembled the woman in the dream, or rather both dream women, one of whom he had stabbed to death and the other who had strangled him with her claws. A shiver of fear ran over his skin. Was all this possibly connected? Was he again being led by unknown spirits? And where to? To Wagner? To murder? To death?

Teresina took his arm as they debarked, and so arm in arm they walked down the bright, noisy quay, through the village and into the casino. There everything had that air of improbability, half exciting, half wearisome, which marks the enterprises of avaricious people transplanted from cities into tranquil landscapes. The buildings were too large and too new, the light too ample, the halls too resplendent, the people too lively. Between the towering, dark mountain ranges and the broad, gentle lake this dense little bee-swarm of greedy and surfeited people squeezed fearfully together, as if uncertain that it could last for another hour, as if at any moment something might happen to wipe it out. From rooms where people were dining and drinking champagne, sickly, fevered violin music sounded. On stairs among palms and leaping fountains massed flowers and women's finery rivalled each other in brilliance. Men's pale faces over open dinner jackets, bustling servants in blue livery with gold buttons, assiduous and knowing, perfumed women with southern faces pale and flushed, beautiful and morbid, and strapping Nordic women, commanding and self-assured, old gentlemen like illustrations for Turgenev and Fontane . . .

Klein felt ill and tired as soon as they entered the casino. In the main hall he took two thousand-franc notes from his pocket.

'What now?' he asked. 'Shall we play together?'

'No, no, that's no fun. Each for himself.'

He gave her one of the notes and asked her to show him what the procedure was. Soon they were standing at a gaming table. Klein placed his banknote on a number, the wheel was turned; he did not know what was going on, merely saw his stake swept away. This goes fast, he thought contentedly, and wanted to smile at Teresina. She was no longer beside him. He saw her standing at another table and changing her money. He went over there. She looked thoughtful, anxious, and very busy, like a housewife.

He followed her to a table and watched her. She was familiar with the game and watched it with close attention. She staked small sums, never more than fifty francs, now here, now there, won several times, tucked notes into her pearl-embroidered handbag and took notes out again.

'How is it going?' he asked at one point.

She was sensitive to interference. 'Oh, let me play. I'll do all right.'

Soon she changed tables. He followed her without her noticing him. Since she was so absorbed and never turned to him for anything, he withdrew to a leather bench along the wall. Solitude descended around him. He began thinking about his dream again. It was very important to understand it. Perhaps he would not have many more such dreams; perhaps, as in fairy tales, they were hints from the good spirits: you were beckoned to twice or thrice, or warned; and if in spite of this you remained as blind as ever, your fate took its course and no friendly power intervened again. From time to time he looked for Teresina, saw her sitting at one table, standing at another. Her yellow hair gleamed brightly among the black dinner jackets.

How long she makes a thousand francs last! he thought, bored. It was faster for me.

Once she nodded in his direction. Once, after an hour, she came over to him, found him abstracted, and placed her hand on his arm.

'What are you doing? Aren't you playing?'

'I have already.'

'Lost?'

'Yes. Oh, it wasn't much.'

'I've won a little. Take some of my money.'

'Thanks, no more today. Are you enjoying yourself?'

'Yes, it's lovely. I'm going back. Or do you want to leave already?'

She went on playing; here and there he saw her hair shining between the shoulders of the players. He brought her a glass of champagne and drank a glass himself. Then he sat down again on the leather bench by the wall.

What was that about the two women in the dream? They had been like his own wife and also the woman in the village tavern and also Teresina. He knew no other women, had not for years. He had stabbed the one woman, revolted by her distorted, swollen face. The other had attacked him from behind and tried to strangle him. Which version was correct? Which was significant? Had he wounded his wife, or she him? Would Teresina destroy him, or he her? Could he not love a woman without inflicting wounds on her and without being wounded by her? Was that his curse? Or was that the general rule? Did it happen to everyone? Was all love like that?

And what linked him to this dancer? That he had fallen in love with her? He had fallen in love with many women without ever saying a word about it. What linked him to her who stood over there engaged in her gambling as if it were a serious business? How childish she was in her eagerness, in her hope; how healthy, naïve, and hungry for life she was! How much would she understand if she knew of his deepest longing, the craving for death, the homesickness for extinction, for return to the bosom of God? Perhaps she would love him, perhaps soon, perhaps she would live with him – but would it be any different from what it had been with his wife? Would he not, for ever and ever, be alone with his deepest feelings?

Teresina interrupted him. She paused in front of him and put a bundle of banknotes into his hand.

'Keep these for me, till later.'

After a while – he did not know whether the time was long or short – she returned and asked for the money.

She's losing, he thought. Thank God! I hope she's finished soon.

Shortly after midnight she returned, pleased and rather flushed. 'So, I'm stopping. Poor man, you must be tired. Should we have a bite to eat before we go home?'

In one of the dining rooms they dined on ham and eggs and fruit, and drank champagne. Klein revived and became lively. The girl was transformed, gay and slightly, sweetly intoxicated. She looked and was aware again that she was beautiful and wearing beautiful clothes; she felt the eyes of the men, courting her from adjacent tables. And Klein, too, felt the change, saw her again in her aura of attractiveness and delicious allurement, heard again the note of provocation and sexuality in her voice, and saw her hands emerging white from the lace, and her neck the colour of pearls.

'How were your winnings?' he asked, laughing.

'Not bad, though not the jackpot yet. Around five thousand.'

'Well, that's nice for a start.'

'Yes, I'm going to continue, of course, next time. But I haven't quite found the right system. It has to come all at once, not in driblets.'

He wanted to say: 'Then you should place your stakes all at once, not in driblets.' But instead he clinked glasses with her and drank to fortune on the grand scale, and laughed and chatted away.

How pretty the girl was, how sound and simple in her pleasure. An hour ago she had been standing at the gaming tables, stern, anxious, with wrinkled brow, angry, calculating. Now she looked as if she had never had a care in the world, as if she knew nothing of money, gambling, business, as though all she knew were pleasure, luxury, and effortless skimming on the iridescent surface of life. Was this all true, all genuine? He himself was also laughing, was amused, was courting joy and love with dancing eyes – and yet at the same time there was a person within him who did not believe in all this, who looked on it all with suspicion and mockery. Was that any different for others? You knew so little, so desperately little about other people. You had learned a hundred dates of ridiculous battles and the names of ridiculous old kings in school; you daily read articles about taxes or about the Balkans; but you knew nothing of people. If a bell failed to ring, if a stove smoked, if a wheel on a machine stuck, you knew at once where to look and did so with alacrity; you found the defect and knew how to cure it. But the thing within you, the secret mainspring that alone gave meaning to life, the thing within us that alone is living, alone is capable of feeling pleasure and pain, of craving happiness and experiencing it – that was unknown. You knew nothing about that, nothing at all, and if the main-spring failed there was no cure. Wasn't it insane?

While he drank and laughed with Teresina, such questions rose and fell in other regions of his mind, now closer to consciousness, now farther away. Everything was doubtful, everything steeped in un-certainties. If only he knew one thing: whether this uncertainty, this distress, this despair in the midst of joy, this compulsion to think and compulsion to question, was present in others also, or whether it was reserved for him alone, for Klein the eccentric?

In one respect, he found, he clearly differed from Teresina; in that respect she was different from him, was childishly and primitively healthy. This girl, like all people and like himself in the past, always in-stinctively reckoned with a future, with tomorrow and the day after, with continuation. Would she otherwise have been able to gamble and to take money so seriously? And here, he felt deeply, he was a different case. For him, behind every feeling and thought was the sense of the open door leading into nothingness. To be sure, he suffered from dread of many things, of madness, the police, insomnia, and also dread of death. But everything he dreaded he likewise desired and longed for at the same time. He was full of burning curiosity about suffering, de-struction, persecution, madness, and death.

'A funny world,' he said under his breath, meaning not the world around him but this inner self. Chatting, they left the casino, walked under the dim lamplight to the sleeping lake shore, where they had to awaken their boatman. It was a while before the boat was ready to leave, and the two stood side by side, transported as if by magic out of the brilliant light and the colourful society of the casino into the dark still-ness of the deserted nocturnal shore, their laughter still on their heated lips but already touched with coolness by night, the imminence of sleep, and fear of loneliness. Both of them felt it. Abruptly, they took each other's hand, smiled wanly and abashedly into the darkness, and each played with dancing fingers on the other's hand and arm. The boatman called, they stepped in, sat down in the cabin, and with a quick movement he drew her blonde head towards him and into the ardour of his kisses.

Fending him off between kisses, she sat up and asked: 'Will we be coming over here again soon?'

In the midst of his erotic stirring, he could not help secretly smiling. With it all she was still thinking of the gambling; she wanted to come back and carry on her business.

'Whenever you like,' he said, wooing her. 'Tomorrow and the day after and every day you wish.'

When he felt her fingers caressing the back of his neck, the memory flashed through him of the terrible feeling in the dream when the vengeful woman clawed at his throat.

'Now she ought to kill me suddenly,' he thought, burning. 'Or I her.'

His groping hand closing around her breast, he laughed softly under his breath. It would have been impossible for him to distinguish pleasure from pain. Even his desire, his hungry longing for embrace with the beautiful, strong woman, could scarcely be distinguished from dread. He longed for her like the condemned man for the axe. Both elements were there, flaming desire and inconsolable grief; both burned, both blazed in fevering stars, both warmed, both killed.

Teresina lithely withdrew from an overbold caress, held both his hands tightly, brought her eyes close to his, and whispered rather absently: 'What kind of man are you, tell me. Why do I love you? Why does something draw me to you? You're old already and not good-looking – how is it? Listen, I do think you're a criminal. Aren't you? Isn't your money stolen?'

He tried to wrest free. 'Don't talk, Teresina! All money is stolen, all property is unjust. Is that important? We are all sinners, we are all criminals, merely because we are alive. Is that important?'

She started. 'Oh, what is important?'

'It's important that we drain this cup,' Klein said slowly. 'Nothing else is important. Perhaps it will never come again. Will you come to my place to sleep, or may I go with you?'

'Come to me,' she said softly. 'I'm afraid of you and yet I must be with you. Don't tell me your secret. I don't want to know anything.'

The sound of the motor throttling down aroused her. She wrenched away from him, smoothed her hair and dress. The boat ran softly up against the landing stage. Bands of lamplight splintered in the black water. They clambered out.

'Wait, my bag!' Teresina exclaimed after they had taken ten steps. She ran back to the stage, jumped into the boat, found the handbag with her money lying on the seat, threw the suspiciously blinking boatman one of the bills, and ran back into the arms of Klein, who was awaiting her on the quay.

Chapter Five

The summer had suddenly begun. In two hot days it had changed the
world, thickened the woods, enchanted the nights. Hour pressed torridly
upon hour; the sun ran swiftly through burning half-circles, the stars
following it hurriedly. A fever of life flared. A silent, greedy haste beset
the world.

An evening came when Teresina's dance in the Rose Garden was
interrupted by furious claps of thunder. The lanterns went out; startled
faces grinned at one another in the white flashes of lightning; women
screamed, waiters shouted, windows rattled.

Klein had at once drawn Teresina over to the table where he sat
beside the old comedian.

'Splendid!' he said. 'Let's go. You're not afraid?'

'No, not afraid. But I won't let you stay with me tonight. You haven't
slept for three nights and you look terrible. Take me home and then go
to your hotel to sleep. Take Veronal if you need it. You're living like a
suicide.'

They left, Teresina in a coat borrowed from a waiter, and tramped
through the wild wind and flashes of lightning and the howling whirls of
dust down streets swept clean. Bright and jubilant, the heavy thunder-
claps boomed through the tumultuous night. Suddenly the rain roared
down, splashing on the pavement, gushing furiously with sobs of release
into the thick summer foliage.

Soaked and shivering, they reached the dancer's apartment. Klein did
not push on to his hotel; nothing more was said of that. With a sigh of

relief they entered the bedroom, laughing, shed their soaked clothes. The glaring flashes of lightning pulsed through the windows; the wind and rain plucked at the acacias.

'We haven't been back to Castiglione yet,' Klein said mockingly. 'When are you going?'

'We'll go again, count on that. Are you bored?'

He drew her close; both were in a fever and the after-glow of the thunderstorm flamed in their embrace. In gusts the chilled air came through the window, with the bitter smell of leaves and the leaden smell of earth. Out of the bodily combat both quickly dropped into slumber. His wasted face lay on the pillow beside her fresh face, his thin, dry hair beside her thick, lovely hair. Outside the window the last flashes of the thunderstorm glimmered, slacked, and ceased. The wind died down. Serenely, a still rain flowed down into the trees.

Soon after one o'clock Klein awoke from a heavy, sultry confusion of dreams – he never slept long any more. His head thudded, his eyes smarted. He lay motionless for a while, eyes wide open, recollecting where he was. It was night, someone was breathing beside him; he was with Teresina.

Slowly, he sat up. Now the torments were coming again; now he was condemned to lie hour upon hour, anguish and dread in his heart, alone, suffering useless pangs, thinking useless thoughts, fretting over useless cares. Out of the nightmares that had awakened him crawled greasy, hulking feelings, disgust and horror, surfeit, self-contempt.

He groped for the light and switched it on. The cool brightness flowed over the white pillow, over chairs heaped with clothes. The gap of the window hung blackly in the narrow wall. Shadows fell over Teresina's averted face; her neck and hair gleamed.

In the past he had sometimes seen his wife lying that way beside him. Sometimes he had also lain sleepless at her side, envying her sleep, feeling mocked by her satiated, contented breathing. Never were you so utterly, so totally abandoned by one closest to you as when that person slept. And again, as so often, there came to his mind the image of the suffering Jesus in the garden of Gethsemane where he was choking with the fear of death but his disciples slept, slept.

Gently, he drew the pillow more to his side, together with Teresina's sleeping head. Now he saw her face, so alien in sleep, so utterly absorbed, so utterly turned away from him. One shoulder and breast lay exposed; under the sheet her abdomen rounded softly with each breath. Odd, he thought, how in speaking of love, in love letters and love poems, people always talked of sweet lips and cheeks, and never of bellies and legs. Fraud! Fraud! He studied Teresina for a long time. With her lovely body, with those breasts and those white, strong, healthy arms and legs, she would still tempt him often and embrace him and derive pleasure from him and then rest and sleep deeply, satiated, without pain, without dread, without foreboding, beautiful and torpid and stupid as a healthy, sleeping animal. And he would lie beside her, sleepless, with fluttering nerves, his heart full of torment? Often? Often? Oh no, no longer often, not many times more, perhaps nevermore. He gave a start. No, he knew it was true: nevermore.

Groaning, he bored his thumb into his eye socket between eye and brow, where these devilish pangs were located. Undoubtedly Wagner had also had these pangs, his teacher Wagner. Surely he had had them, these insane pains, for many years, and had endured them and thought they were making him ripen and bringing him closer to God when all the while they were only useless tortures. Until one day he could no longer endure it – just as he, Klein, could no longer endure it. The pain was the least of it, of course, but the thoughts, the dreams, the nightmares! And then one night Wagner had sprung up and had seen that there was no longer any sense to adding more, many more such nights of torture to one another, that they did not bring him any closer to God, and he had gone for the knife. Perhaps it was pointless, perhaps foolish and ridiculous of Wagner, to have killed. Those who did not know his torments, those who had not suffered his pain, could not understand it, of course.

Only recently he himself had stabbed a woman in a dream because her distorted face had been unbearable to him. But of course everything you loved was distorted, distorted and cruelly provoking when it no longer lied, when it was still, when it slept. Then you looked to the bottom of it and saw no sign of love in it, as you found no sign of love when you looked to the bottom of your own heart. There was only greed for living and dread, and out of dread, out of stupid childish dread of the cold, of loneliness, of death, two people fled to one another, kissed, embraced, rubbed cheek to cheek, put leg to leg, cast new human beings into the world. That was how it was. That was how he had once come to his wife. That was how the innkeeper's wife in a village had come to him, once upon a time, at the beginning of his present course, in a bare stone chamber, barefoot and silent, driven by dread, by greed for living, by need of comfort. That was how he had come to Teresina and she to him. It was always the same instinct, the same craving, the same misunderstanding. And it was also always the same disappointment, the same fierce suffering. You thought you were close to God and held a woman in your arms. You thought you had achieved harmony and had only shifted your guilt and your sorrow to a distant, future being. You held a woman in your arms, kissed her mouth, stroked her breast and begot a child with her, and some day the child would be caught up by the same fate, would likewise lie beside a woman some night and likewise awaken from the frenzy and stare with aching eyes into the abyss and curse the whole thing. Unbearable, to think this thought through to the end.

Attentively, he studied the sleeping girl's face, her shoulder and breast, her yellow hair. All that had delighted him, deceived him, allured him, all that had lied to him of pleasure and happiness. Now it was over, now came the reckoning. He had entered Wagner's theatre; he had realized why every face, as soon as the illusion collapsed, was so distorted and unendurable.

Klein got up from the bed and went to look for a knife. As he stole along he brushed Teresina's long, tan stockings from the chair – and in a flash remembered how he had seen her for the first time, in the park, and how her gait, her shoe, and her taut stocking had sent the first stirrings through him. He laughed softly, with a gloating undertone of malice, and picked Teresina's clothes up piece by piece. He felt them and let them drop to the floor. Then he continued his search, but at moments forgetting everything again. His hat lay on the table; he took it thoughtlessly, turned it in his hands, felt that it was wet, and put it on his head. At the window he paused, looked out into the blackness, heard rain singing; it sounded a note of distant, forgotten times. What did all this mean to him, window, night rain – what concern was it of his, this old picture book of his childhood days.

Suddenly he stood still. He had picked up something that lay on a table, and now he looked at it. It was an oval silver hand mirror, and out of the mirror a face was looking at him, Wagner's face, a madly twisted face with deep, shadowy hollows and shattered, seamed features. It happened so curiously often nowadays that he found himself abruptly looking into a mirror; it seemed to him that earlier he had not looked into one for decades at a time. This, too, it seemed, belonged to the Wagner Theatre.

He stood rigid and gazed into the glass for a long time.

This face belonging to the former Friedrich Klein was done for and used up; it had served its time. Doom screamed out of every furrow. This face must vanish, it must be extinguished. It was very old, this face; far too much had been reflected in it, too much deception, too much dust and rain had passed over it. It had once been smooth and handsome; he had once loved and tended it and taken pleasure in it, and had also often hated it. Why? He could no longer understand either emotion.

And why was he standing here now, at night, in this small, unfamiliar room, with a mirror in his hand and a wet hat on his head – a weird clown. What was the matter with him? What did he want? He sat down on the edge of the table. What had he wanted? What was he looking for? He had been looking for something, something very important.

Oh yes, a knife.

Suddenly horribly shocked, he leaped to his feet and ran to the bed. He stooped over the pillow, saw the sleeping girl lying in her yellow hair. She was still alive! He had not done it yet! Horror flowed icily over him. My God, now it had come! Now he, Wagner, stood by the bed of a sleeping woman and was seeking the knife! No, he would not. No, he was not insane! Thank God he was not insane. Now all was well.

Peace descended upon him. Slowly he dressed, put on his trousers, his jacket, his shoes. Now all was well.

As he was about to step over to the bed once more, he felt something soft underfoot. There lay Teresina's clothing on the floor, the stockings, the light-grey dress. Carefully, he took them up and laid them over the chair.

He put out the light and left the room. Outside, rain was falling, cool and quiet. Nowhere was there a light, nowhere a person, nowhere a sound, only the rain. He turned his face up and let the rain run over his forehead and cheeks. No sky visible. How dark it was. How glad he would have been to see a star.

Quietly, he walked through the streets, soaked by the rain. He met not a soul, not a dog; the world was lifeless. At the lake shore he went from boat to boat. All were drawn far up on land and fastened tightly with chains. Not until he had wandered far into the city's outskirts did he find one that hung loosely on a rope and could be untied. He cast it loose and placed the oars in the oarlocks. Swiftly, the shore vanished; it fell away into greyness as if it had never been. Only greyness and blackness and rain remained in the world, grey water, wet water, grey lake, wet sky, all of it without end.

Far out in the lake, he drew in the oars. The time had come, and he was content. Formerly, at moments when dying seemed inevitable to him, he had always gladly delayed a little longer, postponed the thing until the next day, given living one more try. There was no more of that.

His little boat, that was it, was his small, limited, artificially guarded life – but the expanse of greyness all around was the world, was the universe and God. It was not hard to let himself drop into that; it was easy, it was gladdening.

He sat on the edge of the boat with his feet dangling into the water. Slowly he leaned forward, leaned forward, until the boat behind him slid briskly away. He was in the universe.

Into the small number of moments he continued to live, far more experience was packed than into the forty years in which he had been on the way to this goal.

It began this way: at the moment he fell, when for the fraction of a second he hung between the edge of the boat and the water, it came to him that he was committing suicide, a piece of childishness, something not bad, certainly, but comical and rather foolish. The pathos of wanting to die and the pathos of dying itself coalesced within him. It amounted to nothing. His dying was not necessary, not any more. It was desirable, it was fine and welcome, but it was no longer necessary. Since that flashing fraction of a second in which he had let himself drop from the side of the boat with his whole volition, with complete renunciation of all volition, with total surrender, dropping into the maternal womb, into the arm of God – since that moment dying had ceased to have any meaning. It was all so simple, all so wonderfully easy, after all; there were no longer any abysses, any difficulties. The whole trick was to let yourself go. That thought shone through his whole being as the result of his life: let yourself go. Once you did that, once you had given up, yielded, surrendered, renounced all props and all firm ground underfoot, once you listened solely to the counsel in your own heart, everything was gained. Then everything was good, there was no longer any dread, no longer any danger.

This was achieved, this great thing, this only thing: he had let himself fall. That he was letting himself fall into water and into death would not have been necessary; he could just as well have let himself fall into life. But that did not matter much, was not important. He would live, he would come again. But then he would no longer need suicide or any of these strange detours, any of these toilsome and painful follies, for then he would have overcome the dread.

Wonderful thought: a life without dread! To overcome dread: that was bliss, that was redemption. How he had suffered from dread all his life, and now, when death already had him by the throat, he no longer felt it, no dread, no horror, only smiles, release, consent. He suddenly knew what dread was, and that it could be overcome only by one who recognized it. You dreaded a thousand things, pain, judgement, your own heart. You felt dread of sleep, dread of awakening, of being alone, of cold, of madness, of death – especially of that, of death. But all these were only masks and disguises. In reality there was only one thing you dreaded: letting yourself fall, taking the step into uncertainty, the little step beyond all the securities that existed. And whoever had once surrendered himself, one single time, whoever had practised the great act of confidence and entrusted himself to fate, was liberated. He no longer obeyed the laws of earth; he had fallen into space and swung along in the dance of the constellations. That was it. It was so simple. Every child could understand that, could know that.

He did not think this as one thinks thoughts. He lived, felt, touched, smelled, and tasted it. He tasted, smelled, saw, and understood what life was. He saw the creation of the world and saw the downfall of the world, like two armies moving in opposite directions, never stopping, eternally on the march. The world was constantly being born and constantly dying. All life was a breath exhaled by God. All dying was a breath inhaled by God. One who had learned not to resist, to let himself fall, died easily, was born easily. One who resisted, who suffered dread, died hard, was born reluctantly.

In the grey darkness of the rain above the nocturnal lake the drowning man saw the drama of the world mirrored and represented: suns and stars rolled up, rolled down; choirs of men and animals, spirits and angels, stood facing one another, sang, fell silent, shouted; processions of living beings marched towards one another, each misunderstanding himself, hating himself, and hating and persecuting himself in every other being. All of them yearned for death, for peace; their goal was God, was the return to God and remaining in God. This goal created dread, for it was an error. There was no remaining in God. There was no peace. There was only the eternal, eternal, glorious, holy being exhaled and inhaled, assuming form and being dissolved, birth and death, exodus and return, without pause, without end. And therefore there was only one art, only one teaching, only one secret: to let yourself fall, not to resist God's will, to cling to nothing, neither to good nor to evil. Then you were redeemed, then you were free of suffering, free of dread – only then.

His life lay before him like a landscape with woods, valleys, and villages that could be viewed from the ridge of a high mountain range. Everything had been good, simple and good, and everything had been converted by his dread, by his resisting, to torment and complexity, to horrible knots and convulsions of wretchedness and grief. There was no woman you could not live without – and there also was no woman with whom you could not have lived. There was not a thing in the world that was not just as beautiful, just as desirable, just as joyous as its opposite. It was blissful to live, it was blissful to die, as soon as you hung suspended alone in space. Peace from without did not exist; there was no peace in the graveyard, no peace in God. No magic ever interrupted the eternal chain of births, the endless succession of God's breaths. But there was another kind of peace, to be found within your own self. Its name was: Let yourself fall! Do not fight back! Die gladly! Live gladly!

All the figures of his life were with him, all the faces of his love, all the guises of his suffering. His wife was pure and as guiltless as himself. Teresina smiled childishly. The murderer Wagner, whose shadow had fallen so heavily across Klein's life, smiled earnestly into his face, and his smile said that Wagner's act, too, had been one way to redemption; it too had been breath, it too a symbol, and that even killing and blood and atrocities were not things that truly existed, but only assessments of our own self-tormenting souls. He, Klein, had spent years of his life dealing with Wagner's murder, rejecting and approving, condemning and admiring, despising and imitating. Out of this murder he had created endless chains of torments, dreads, miseries. A hundred times, full of dread, he had attended his own death, had seen himself dying on the scaffold, had felt the razor blade cutting into his own throat and the bullet in his own temple – and now that he was dying the death he had feared, it was so easy, so simple, was joy and triumph. Nothing in the world need be feared, nothing was terrible – only in our delusions do we create all this fear, all this suffering for ourselves, only in our own frightened souls do good and evil, worth and worthlessness, craving and fear arise.

The figure of Wagner vanished far in the distance. He was not Wagner, no longer; there was no Wagner. All that had been illusion. Let Wagner die now! He, Klein, would live.

Water flowed into his mouth and he drank. From all sides, through all his senses, water flowed in; everything dissolved in it. He was being drawn, breathed in. Beside him, pressed against him, as close together as the drops of water, floated other people; Teresina floated, the old comedian floated, his wife, his father, his mother and sister, and thousands, thousands, thousands of others, and pictures and buildings as well, Titian's Venus and Strasbourg Cathedral, everything floated, pressed close together, in a tremendous stream, driven by necessity, faster and faster, rushing madly – and this tremendous, gigantic, raging stream of forms was racing towards another stream just as vast, racing just as fast, a stream of faces, legs, bellies, animals, flowers, thoughts, murders, suicides, written books, wept tears, dense, dense, full, full, children's eyes and black curls and fishheads, a woman with a long rigid knife in her bloody belly, a young man resembling himself, face full of holy passion, that was himself at the age of twenty, that vanished Klein of the past. How good that this insight too was coming to him now: that there was no time! The only thing that stood between old age and youth, between Babylon and Berlin, between good and evil, giving and taking, the only thing that filled the world with differences, opinions, suffering, conflict, war, was the human mind, the young, tempestuous, and cruel human mind in the stage of rash youth, still far from knowledge, still far from God. That mind invented contradictions, invented names; it called some things beautiful, some ugly, some good, some bad. One part of life was called love, another murder. How young, foolish, comical this mind was. One of its inventions was time. A subtle invention, a refined instrument for torturing the self even more keenly and making the world multiplex and difficult. For then man was separated from all he craved only by time, by time alone, this crazy invention! It was one of the props, one of the crutches that you had to let go, that one above all, if you wanted to be free.

The universal stream of forms flowed on, the forms inhaled by God and the other, the contrary forms that he breathed out. Klein saw those who opposed the current, who reared up in fearful convulsions and created horrible tortures for themselves: heroes, criminals, madmen, thinkers, lovers, religious. He saw others like himself being carried along swiftly and easily, in the deep voluptuousness of yielding, of consent. Blessed like himself. Out of the song of the blessed and out of the endless cries of torment from the unblessed there rose over both universal streams a transparent sphere or dome of sound, a cathedral of music. In its midst sat God, a bright star, invisible from sheer brightness, the quintessence of light, with the music of the universal choirs roaring around in eternal surges.

Heroes and thinkers emerged from the universal stream, prophets. 'Behold, this is God the Lord and his way leads to peace,' one of them cried, and many followed him. Another proclaimed that God's path led to struggle and war. One called him light, one night, one father, one mother. One praised him as tranquillity, one as movement, as fire, as coal, as judge, as comforter, as creator, as destroyer, as forgiver, as avenger. God himself did not call himself anything. He wanted to be called, wanted to be loved, wanted to be praised, cursed, hated, worshipped, for the music of the universal choirs was his temple and was his life – but he did not care what names were used to hail him, whether he was loved or hated, whether men sought rest and sleep or dance and furore in him. Everyone could seek. Everyone could find.

Now Klein heard his own voice. He was singing. With a new, mighty, high, reverberating voice he sang loudly, loudly and resoundingly sang God's praise. He sang as he floated along in the rushing stream in the midst of the millions of creatures. He had become a prophet and proclaimer. Loudly, his song resounded; the vault of music rose high; radiantly, God sat within it. The streams roared tremendously along.

Klingsor's Last Summer

Preface

The painter Klingsor spent the last summer of his life, at the age of forty-two, in those southerly regions in the vicinity of Pampambio, Kareno, and Laguno which he had loved in earlier years and often visited. There his last paintings were done, those free paraphrases on the forms of the world of phenomena, those strange, glowing, and yet dreamily tranquil pictures with their twisted trees and plantlike houses which connoisseurs prefer to the works of his 'classical' period. At the time his palette had been reduced to a few, extremely vivid colours: cadmium yellow and red, Veronese green, emerald, cobalt, cobalt-violet, French vermilion, and crimson lake.

In late fall the news of Klingsor's death shocked his friends. Many of his letters had contained forebodings or death wishes. This may have nourished the rumour that he had taken his own life. Other rumours, such as always gather around a controversial name, have as little substance as that one. Many asserted that Klingsor had been mentally ill during his last months, and a somewhat myopic art critic attempted to explain the startling and ecstatic quality of his last paintings on the grounds of this alleged madness! That is all nonsense. There is somewhat more foundation to the story – which has been embroidered with a wealth of anecdotes – of Klingsor's heavy drinking. He certainly had this tendency, and no one spoke of it more frankly than Klingsor himself. At certain times in his life, and therefore during his last months also, it was more than a case of frequent drinking bouts. He would also deliberately drown his pain and his sometimes almost unbearable melancholy in wine. Li Po, that author of the profoundest drinking songs, was his favourite, and in his cups he often called himself Li Po and one of his friends Tu Fu.

His works live. And among the small circle of his intimates the legend of his life and of that last summer lives on no less forcefully.

Klingsor

A passionate summer of swift-moving life had begun. The hot days, long as they were, flared up and away like burning streamers. The brief sultry moonlit nights were followed by brief sultry rainy nights. Swift as dreams crowded with images, the glittering weeks moved feverishly on.

Just back home after a night walk, Klingsor stood on the narrow stone balcony of his studio. Below him, dizzyingly precipitate, the old terrace gardens dropped away, a densely shadowed tangle of treetops, palms, cedars, chestnuts, judas trees, red beech, and eucalyptus, intertwined with climbing plants, lianas, wisterias. Above the blackness of the trees the large glossy leaves of the summer magnolias gleamed pallidly, the huge snow-white blossoms half-shut among them, large as human heads, pale as moon and ivory. From the massed leafage, penetrating and rousing, a tartly sweet smell of lemons drifted towards him. From some indefinite distance languorous music winged its way to him, perhaps a guitar, perhaps a piano; there was no saying. A peacock suddenly cried from a yard, twice, three times, piercing the silvan night with the short, angry, wooden tone of its tormented voice, as if the pain of the whole animal world were sounding shrilly, coarsely from the depths. Starlight flowed through the wooded valley. High and deserted, a white chapel, enchanted and old, peered out of the endless forest. In the distance lake, mountains, and sky flowed together.

Klingsor stood on the balcony, coatless, his bare forearms leaning on the iron railing, and with a touch of sullenness, his eyes hot, read the script of the stars against the pale sky and the gentle lucency on the black, lumpy cloud masses of the trees. The peacock reminded him. Yes, it was night again, late, and he ought to go to sleep now, absolutely and at all costs. Perhaps, if he could really sleep for several nights in succession, sleep soundly for six or eight hours, he would be able to recover, his eyes would be obedient and patient again, his heart calmer and his temples without pain. But then this summer would be over, this crazy, flickering summer dream, and along with it a thousand undrunk glasses would be spilled, a thousand unseen loving looks shattered, a thousand irrecoverable pictures extinguished unseen!

He laid his forehead and his aching eyes against the cool iron railing. That refreshed him for a moment. In a year perhaps, or sooner, these eyes would be blind and the fires in his heart extinct. No, no human being could endure his flaming life for long. Not even he could, not even Klingsor, who had ten lives. Nobody could go on for a long time having all his candles burning day and night, all his volcanoes flaming. Nobody could be ablaze day and night, working feverishly for many hours every day, spending many hours every night in feverish thoughts, forever enjoying, forever creating, forever with all his senses and nerves wide awake and alert, like a palace behind whose every window music rings out day after day, while night after night a thousand candles twinkle. It would come to an end. A great deal of strength had already been squandered, much eyesight consumed, much life bled away.

Suddenly he laughed and stretched. He remembered that he had often before felt like this, often before thought these thoughts, had these fears. In all the good, fruitful, and ardent periods of his life, even in his youth, he had lived like this, had burned his candle at both ends, with a half jubilant, half mournful feeling of wild extravagance, of burning himself up, with a desperate greed to empty the cup to the dregs, and with a deep, hidden dread of the end. Often before he had lived like this, often drained the cup, often burned with high, darting flames. Sometimes these spells had ended gently, in something like a deep, unconscious hibernation. Sometimes the letdown had been terrible, senseless devastation, intolerable pain, doctors, sad renunciations, victory of weakness. And, granted, each time the end of such a period of intensity had been progressively worse, blacker, more shattering. However, he had always survived these lows and after weeks or months, after agony or stupefaction, the resurrection had come, new fire, new eruption of the underground volcanoes, new and more passionate works, new, glittering frenzy. That was how it had been, and the times of torment and subsidence, the agonizing intervals, had been forgotten and had vanished. It was good that way. This time, too, it would go as it had often gone.

Smiling, he thought of Gina, whom he had seen this evening, around whom his thoughts had revolved affectionately all the long walk home through the night. How beautiful this girl was, and how warm in her still inexperienced and timorous ardour. Playfully and tenderly he murmured under his breath, as if he were again whispering into her ear: 'Gina! Gina! *Cara* Gina! *Carina* Gina! *Bella* Gina!'

He stepped back into the room and turned the light on again. From a small, haphazard heap of books he took a volume of poems. A poem had come to his mind, a fragment of a poem which seemed to him inexpressibly lovely. He searched for a long time before he found it:

Do not leave me to my sorrow now,
Beloved, do not leave me to the night.
Oh, you who are my match, who are my candle,
You who are my sun, who are my light.

With deep enjoyment he sipped the dark wine of these words. How lovely, how tender and magical it was: Oh, you who are my candle. And: You who are my sun.

Smiling, he paced back and forth in front of the tall windows, reciting the verses, calling them out to the distant Gina: 'Oh, you who are my light!' His voice darkened with tenderness.

Then he opened the portfolio he had carried with him all evening after his long day of work. He opened the sketchbook, looked at the last pages, the ones he had done yesterday and today. There was the cone-shaped mountain with the deep shadows of cliffs; he had rendered it so it looked very like a crazy masked face. The mountain seemed to be screaming, splitting open from pain. There was the small stone fountain, a semicircle on the mountain slope, the masonry arch filled with black shadows, a flowering pomegranate tree blazing above it. It was all there for him alone to read, a cipher for himself, hasty, greedy notation of the instant, swiftly snatched recollection of every moment in which nature and his heart sounded newly and loudly in concord. And now came the larger coloured sketches, white sheets with luminous areas of watercolour: the red villa in the woods, with a fiery glow like a ruby on green velvet, and the iron bridge at Castiglia, red against the blue-green mountain, the violet dam beside it and the pink road. Further: the chimney of the brickworks, red rocket against light, cool tree-green, blue signpost, brilliant violet sky with the thick cloud like rolled steel. This sheet was good; it could stay. Things had gone less well with the wagon road to the stable; the reddish-brown against the steely sky was right, it spoke and sounded, but the picture was only half finished. The sun had shone on the paper and made his eyes ache maddeningly. For a long while afterwards he had bathed his face in a brook. Well, the brown-red against the malignant metallic blue was there; that was good, there was not the smallest nuance, not the slightest vibration wrong or off. Without Indian red he couldn't have brought that off. There, in this field, lay the secrets. The forms of nature, their top and bottom, their thick and thin, could be shifted around; you could discard all the commonplace means for imitating nature. You could falsify colours too, of course; you could intensify, lower, translate them in a hundred different ways. But if you wanted to use colour to create a fictional nature, what mattered was that the few colours stood exactly, with the utmost exactitude, in the same relationships, in the same tensions to one another as they did in nature. Here you remained dependent, here you remained a naturalist, even though you took orange instead of grey and carmine instead of black.

So then, another day had been squandered and the yield was meagre. The study of the factory chimney and the jotting in red and blue and perhaps the sketch of the fountain. If it were a cloudy day tomorrow he would go to Carabbina; there was that portico where the women came to do their laundry. Perhaps it would rain again tomorrow; then he would stay home and begin working on the picture of the brook in oils. And now to bed. It was past one o'clock again.

In the bedroom he pulled off his shirt, slapped water over his shoulders so that it dripped down on the red tile floor, jumped into the high bed, and put out the light. Pale Monte Salute looked in through the window. A thousand times Klingsor had traced its forms from his bed. An owl cried from the wooded gorge, deep and hollow, like sleep, like forgetfulness.

He closed his eyes and thought of Gina, and of the portico with the washtubs. God in heaven, so many thousands of things were waiting, so many thousands of cups stood ready poured. Not a thing on earth that he should not have painted. Not a woman in the world whom he should not have loved. Why did time exist? Why always this idiotic succession of one thing after another, and not a roaring, surfeiting simultaneity? Why was he now lying alone in bed again, like a widower, like an old man? You could enjoy, could create, all through this short life; and yet at best you were always merely singing one song after another. The whole full symphony with all its hundred voices and instruments never sounded all at once.

Long ago, at the age of twelve, he had been Klingsor with the ten lives. The boys played a game of robbers, and each of the robbers had ten lives. Each time you were tagged by your opponent or touched by his thrown javelin, you lost one life. But the game went on as long as you had six, three, even one single life left. Only when you lost the tenth were you out. But he, Klingsor, had made it a matter of pride to win through without losing any of his ten lives and would consider himself disgraced if he came out with nine or with seven. That was how he had been as a boy, in that incredible period when nothing in the world was impossible, nothing in the world was difficult, when everybody loved Klingsor, when Klingsor commanded everyone, when everything belonged to Klingsor. And that was how he had gone on, always living with ten lives. And although the surfeit, the full roaring symphony, could never be attained – still his song had not been single-voiced and impoverished. He had always had a few more strings to his bow than others, a few more irons in the fire, a few more coins in his purse, a few more horses on his cart. Thank God!

How full and vibrant the dark stillness of the garden was, like the breathing of a sleeping woman. How the peacock screeched. How the fire burned in his breast, how his heart pounded and cried and suffered and rejoiced and bled. It had been a good summer after all up here in Castagnetta. He lived gloriously in his noble old ruin, looked gloriously out on the caterpillar backs of the innumerable chestnut groves below. It was lovely to descend eagerly now and then from this noble old world of woods and castles and look at the gay colourful toys down below and paint them in their good gay gaudiness: the factory, the railroad, the blue streetcars, the advertising column by the dock, the strutting peacocks, women, priests, automobiles. And how lovely and tormenting and incomprehensible was this feeling in his breast, this love and flickering craving for every bright ribbon and rag of life, this wild sweet compulsion to see and to shape, and yet secretly at the same time, under thin lids, the deep-felt knowledge of the childishness and vanity of all he did.

Fevered, the brief summer night melted away. Vapour rose from the green depths of the valley, sap simmered in a hundred thousand trees, a hundred thousand dreams swelled up in Klingsor's light slumber, his soul strode through his life's hall of mirrors where all images were mul-

tiplied and each time met one another with new faces and new meanings and entered into new associations, as though a firmament were
being shaken in a dice cup.

One dream image among the many delighted and greatly stirred him.
He lay in a forest and had a woman with red hair across his lap, and a
black-haired woman leaned against his shoulder, and another knelt beside him, holding his hand and kissing his fingers, and everywhere, all
around, were women and girls, some still children, with long thin legs,
some nubile, some mature and with the signs of knowledge and of
fatigue in their restive faces, and all loved him and all wanted to be
loved by him. Then war and fury erupted among the women, the red
one thrust a raging hand into the black one's hair and pulled her to the
ground and was herself dragged down, and all fell upon one another,
each one screaming, each tearing, each biting, each hurting, each suffering pain. Laughter, cries of fury and howls of anguish rang out intertwined and tangled, blood flowed everywhere, nails dug bloodily into
fat flesh.

With a feeling of sorrow and depression Klingsor awoke for a few
minutes. His eyes, wide open, stared at the bright gap in the wall. The
faces of the embattled women still lingered, and he recognized and
named many of them: Nina, Hermine, Elizabeth, Gina, Edith, Berta,
and in a hoarse voice, still caught up in the dream, he said: 'Children,
stop it! You're lying you know, you're deceiving me, you know; it's not
each other you should be tearing to pieces but me, me!'

Louis

Louis the Cruel had dropped out of the blue. Suddenly he was there, Klingsor's old friend, the traveller, the unpredictable wanderer who lived in railroad cars and whose studio was his knapsack. Good times dripped out of the blue on these days, good winds came. They painted together, on the Mount of Olives and in Cartago.

'I wonder whether all this painting business has any real value,' Louis said on the Mount of Olives, lying naked in the grass, his back red from the sun. 'You know we only paint for lack of anything better to do, my friend. If you always had the girl you like best on your lap at the moment and your favourite soup in your plate, you wouldn't bother with this senseless childish game. Nature has ten thousand colours and we've taken it into our heads to reduce the spectrum to twenty. That's what painting is. We're never satisfied and on top of everything else we have to help the critics earn their livings. On the other hand, a good Marseilles bouillabaisse, *caro mio*, and a simple lukewarm Burgundy along with it, and afterwards a piccata Milanese, pears and Gorgonzola for dessert, and Turkish coffee – those are realities, dear sir, those are values! How badly people eat in your Palestine here! Ah, I wish I were in a cherry tree and the cherries were growing into my mouth and just above me on the ladder stood the sun-tanned, spirited girl we met this morning. Klingsor, give up painting! I'm inviting you to a good meal in Laguno. It's getting to be about time.'

'Do you mean it?' Klingsor asked, screwing up his eyes.

'I mean it. Only first I have to hurry over to the station. You see, to be truthful, I've telegraphed a woman friend that I am dying. She may arrive by the eleven o'clock train.'

Laughing, Klingsor tore the unfinished study off his easel.

'You're right, my boy. Let us go to Laguno! Put on your shirt, Luigi. There's great innocence to the morals here, but unfortunately you cannot go into town naked.'

They went into town, they went to the station; a beautiful woman arrived; they ate well in a restaurant and Klingsor, who had forgotten during his months in the country, was astonished that all these things still existed, these dear, cheerful things: trout, smoked ham, asparagus, Chablis, Valais Dôle, Benedictine.

After the meal all three of them took the cable railway up through the steep city, passing right between the houses, by windows and hanging gardens. It was very pretty. They stayed in their seats and rode down again, and up and down still again. The world was strangely beautiful and rare, highly colourful, somewhat dubious, somewhat improbable, but lovely. But Klingsor was a bit embarrassed; he put on an air of indifference, for he did not want to fall in love with Luigi's beautiful friend. They dropped in at a café, they walked in the park, deserted in the afternoon heat, they lay down by the water under the huge trees. They saw a great deal that deserved to be painted: red houses like gems set in deep green, snakewood trees and smoke trees seared blue and brown.

'You have painted delightful and jolly things, Luigi,' Klingsor said, 'things I'm very fond of: flagpoles, clowns, circuses. But to me, the most precious of all is a spot on your picture of the carousel after dark. You know, high up in the night, far above the violet tent and far from all the lights is a cool, small flag, pale pink, so beautiful, so cool, so lonely, so horribly lonely! It's like a poem by Li Po or Paul Verlaine. All the sorrow and all the resignation of the world is in that small, silly pink flag, and all good laughter at sorrow and resignation. Your life is justified for having painted that little flag. I count it one of your major achievements, that flag.'

'Yes, I know how you like it.'

'You like it yourself. Look, if you hadn't painted a few such things, all the good food and wine and women and coffee would do you little good, you'd be a poor devil. But as it is you're a rich devil and a hell of a good fellow whom people are fond of. You know, Luigi, I often think as you do: that all our art is merely a substitute, a painful substitute bought ten times too dearly for missed life, missed animality, missed love. But it really isn't so. It's altogether different. If we regard the things of the mind as merely paltry substitutes for missing sensuality, we're overestimating the things of the senses. Sensuality isn't worth a hair more than spirituality, and it's the same the other way around. It's all one, everything is equally good. Whether you embrace a woman or make a poem, it's the same. So long as the main thing is there, the love, the burning, the emotion, it doesn't matter whether you are a monk on Mount Athos or a man about town in Paris.'

Louis looked slowly across at him, his eyes mocking. 'My boy, you're gettin' too fancy for me.'

They roamed the vicinity with their beautiful companion. Both of them were good at seeing; that they could do. Within the circuit of a few towns and villages they saw Rome, Japan, the South Seas, and rubbed out the illusions again with sportive fingers. Their whims kindled stars in the sky and extinguished them again. Through the lush nights they sent their globes of light rising. The world was a soap bubble, opera, joyous nonsense.

Louis the Bird flew on his bicycle through the hilly landscape, went here and there while Klingsor painted. Klingsor threw away a good many days; then again he would sit resolutely outside and work. Louis did not want to work. Louis left all of a sudden, together with his woman friend; he sent a postcard from far away. Suddenly he was back, when Klingsor had already given him up for lost. He stood at the door in straw hat and open shirt as if he had never been away. Once again Klingsor drained the drink of friendship from the sweetest cup of his youth. He had many friends, many loved him; he had given much to many, opened his impulsive heart to many. But this summer only two of his friends heard the old cry of his heart fall from his lips: the painter Louis and the writer Hermann, called Tu Fu.

Many a day Louis sat in the field on his painting stool, in the shade of the pear tree, in the shade of the plum tree, and did not paint. He sat and thought, kept paper clipped to the easel and wrote, wrote a great deal, wrote many letters. Are people who write so many letters happy? He wrote strenuously, Louis the Nonchalant; for hours at a time his eyes clung devotedly to the paper. Much that he concealed churned within him. Klingsor loved him for that.

Klingsor behaved differently. He could not keep silent. He could not conceal what lay in his heart. He let his intimates know the secret pangs of his life. Often he suffered from anxiety, from melancholia; often he

lay bound and gagged in the dungeon of darkness. Sometimes shadows
from his earlier life fell upon his days, casting them in gloom. Then it
did him good to see Luigi's face. Then, sometimes, he would vent his
feelings to him.

But Louis did not like to see these weaknesses. They pained him, they
demanded sympathy. Klingsor made it a practice to reveal his heart to
his friend, and realized too late that in so doing he was losing him.

Again Louis began to talk of departure. Klingsor knew that he would
be able to hold him only for a few days, for three, perhaps five. Then
suddenly Louis would show him his packed suitcases and leave, and
not be back for a long time. How short life was, how irrevocable everything was. Louis was the only one of his friends who fully understood
his art, whose own art was close to his and equal to it. Now he had
spoiled things with this only friend, had chilled him and put him out
of sorts, merely out of stupid infirmity and slackness, merely out of the
childish and unseemly impulse to spare himself trouble, to keep no
secrets, to throw aside dignity. How silly, how boyish that had been.
Thus Klingsor berated himself – too late.

On the last day they tramped together through the golden valleys.
Louis was in excellent humour; departure was the spring of life to his
migratory bird's heart. Klingsor fell in with his mood. Once again they
had found the old, easy, playful and mocking tone, and this time they
did not let it slip. In the evening they sat in the tavern garden. They
had fish baked specially for them, had rice with mushrooms to go with
it, and poured maraschino over peaches.

'Where are you bound for tomorrow?' Klingsor asked.

'I don't know.'

'Are you going to join that beautiful woman?'

'Yes. Perhaps. Who can tell? Don't ask too many questions. Now, at
the end, let's have another good white wine. I'm in favour of a Neuchâtel.'

They drank. Suddenly Louis exclaimed: 'It's a good thing I'm
leaving, old seal. Sometimes, when I sit beside you like this, like now,
for instance, something utterly silly occurs to me. It occurs to me that
here and now the only two painters our good country can boast of are
sitting together, and then I have a horrible feeling in my knees, as if
the two of us were cast in bronze and standing hand in hand on a
monument, you know, like Goethe and Schiller. After all, it's not their
fault that they're condemned to stand there forever holding each other's
bronze hands and that they gradually come to seem so odious and such
a damned nuisance to us. Maybe they were perfectly decent fellows –

years ago I read a play by Schiller that was pretty good. And yet this is what's happened to him now, he's become a monument and has to stand beside his Siamese twin and you see their collected works standing on shelves and hear them analysed in the schools. It's gruesome. Imagine a professor a hundred years from now preaching to his students: Klingsor, born in 1877, and his contemporary Louis, nicknamed The Glutton, innovators in painting, liberation from the naturalism of colour, when we examine this pair of artists closely we find three clearly distinguishable periods! I'd rather throw myself under a locomotive right here and now!'

'It would make more sense to throw the professors under it.'

'There aren't any locomotives that big. Our technology is so small scale.'

Stars were already rising. Suddenly Louis clinked glasses with his friend.

'All right, one more toast and let's drink it down. Then I'll mount my wheel and goodbye. Let's not have any long partings. Cheers, Klingsor!'

They touched glasses and drank. In the garden Louis mounted his bicycle, swung his hat, was gone. Night, stars. Louis was in China, Louis was a legend.

Klingsor smiled sadly. How he loved this migratory bird! For a long time he stood on the gravel in the tavern garden, gazing down the empty street.

The Day at Kareno

Together with his friends from Barengo and with Agosto and Ersilia Klingsor set out on the walk to Kareno. Early in the morning they descended among the strongly scented spireas, the bedewed spider-webs quivering on the margins of the woods, down through the steep, warm forest into the valley of Pampambio where beside the yellow road bright yellow houses slept, bent forward and half dead, stunned by the summer days. By the dried-up stream bed the white metallic willows hung heavy wings over golden meadows. A colourful troupe, the friends bowled down the rosy road through the misty green of the valley: the men white and yellow in linens and silks, the women white and pink, Ersilia's Veronese green parasol sparkling like a jewel in a magic ring.

'It's a pity, Klingsor,' the doctor remarked plaintively in his kindly voice. 'Your wonderful watercolours will all be white in ten years. These colours you like so well have no lasting qualities.'

'Yes,' Klingsor said, 'and what is worse, Doctor: your fine brown hair will all be grey in ten years, and a little while later all our good gay bones will be lying in some hole in the ground, including, alas, your beautiful and healthy bones, Ersilia. My friends, let's not start becoming sensible so late in life. Hermann, how does Li Po put it?'

Hermann the Poet stood still and intoned:

Life passes like a flash of lightning
Whose blaze barely lasts long enough to see.
While the earth and the sky stand still forever

How swiftly changing time flies across man's face.
O you who sit over your full cup and do not drink,
Tell me whom you are still waiting for?

'No,' Klingsor said, 'I mean the other poem, the rhymed one, about the hair that was still dark at morning . . .'
Hermann promptly recited:

Only this morning your hair gleamed silken and black,
Evening has already sprinkled it with snow.
If you would not suffer as on the rack
Hold out your cup and summon the moon for your drink-fellow.

Klingsor laughed heartily in his somewhat hoarse voice.
'Good old Li Po! He had inklings; he knew all sorts of things. We know all sorts of things too – he is our wise old brother. This giddy day would please him. It's just the kind of day lovely for dying Li Po's death at evening, in the boat on the quiet river. You'll see, everything is going to be wonderful today.'
'What kind of death was it that Li Po died on the river?' Martha, the artist, asked.
But Ersilia interrupted in her dear, deep voice: 'Stop it now. I'll begin detesting anybody who says another word about death and dying. *Finisca adesso, brutto* Klingsor!'
Laughing, Klingsor came over to her. 'How right you are, *bambina*! If I say another word about dying you can poke your parasol into both my eyes. But seriously, 'tis a glorious day, my dears. A bird is singing today, a bird out of a fairy tale – I heard it once before this morning. A wind is blowing today, a wind out of a fairy tale, the child of heaven who wakens the sleeping princesses and blows reason clear out of people's heads. A flower is blossoming today, a flower out of a fairy tale, it's blue and blooms only once in a lifetime and whoever plucks it wins bliss.'
'Did all that mean anything?' Ersilia asked the doctor.
Klingsor heard her.
'What it all meant is: this day will never come again and anyone who fails to eat and drink and taste and smell it will never have it offered to him again in all eternity. The sun will never shine as it does today; it is in a constellation in the sky, a conjunction with Jupiter, with me, with

Agosto and Ersilia and all of us, a conjunction that will never come
again, not in a thousand years. And therefore I want to walk on your
left side for a while, because that brings luck, and carry your emerald
parasol – under its light my head will look like an opal. But you must
play your part and sing a song, one of your best.'

He took Ersilia's arm. His sharp features dipped softly into the blue-
green shade of the parasol. He had fallen in love with it; its blatant,
sweet colour delighted him.

Ersilia began to sing:

> *Il mio papà no vuole,*
> *Ch'io spos' un bersaglier—*

Voices joined in; singing, they walked on to the forest and into the
forest, until the climb became too steep. The path led sharply upward
like a ladder, scaling the great mountain.

'What a marvellous straight line this song takes!' Klingsor praised
it. 'Papa is against the lovers, just as he always is. They take a knife that
cuts well and stab Papa to death. He's gone. They do it at night, nobody sees them but the moon, who doesn't betray them, and the stars,
who are mute, and God, who's going to forgive them after all. How
beautiful and sincere that is. A poet of the present day would be stoned
for writing such a thing.'

They climbed the narrow mountain path in the sun-splashed
shadows of the chestnuts. When Klingsor looked up he saw before his
face the slender calves of Martha, the artist, showing pink through her
transparent stockings. If he looked back, the green of the parasol
arched above Ersilia's curly black hair. Underneath she was silken
violet, the only dark patch among all these figures.

At a blue and orange farmhouse fallen summer apples lay in the
meadow, cool and sour. They tasted them. Martha spoke enthusiastic-
ally about an outing on the Seine, in Paris, before the war. Ah yes, Paris,
and the bliss of those days.

'That will never come again. Never again.'

'Nor ought it to,' the painter exclaimed vehemently, shaking his
sparrow-hawk's head fiercely. 'Nothing ought to come again. Why
should it? What childish wishes! The war has glossed over everything
in the past, turning it all into a paradise, even the most idiotic things,
the things we could well do without. Very well, it was lovely in Paris and
lovely in Rome and lovely in Arles. But is it any less lovely today, right

here? Paradise isn't Paris and peacetime, Paradise is here. It lives up there on the mountain and in an hour we'll be in the midst of it and will be the thieves to whom it was said: This day you will be with me in Paradise.'

They broke out of the mottled shade of the wood's path on to the broad open highway that soared, bright and hot, in great spirals to the summit. Klingsor, his eyes shielded by his dark-green glasses, walked last in line, and often fell behind to watch the others moving and see the coloured combinations they formed. He had deliberately taken nothing with him for working, not even his small notebook; and nevertheless he stood still a hundred times, stirred by pictures. His gaunt figure stood alone, showing white against the reddish gravel of the road, at the edge of a grove of acacias. Summer breathed hotly upon the mountain. Light poured vertically down. Colour steamed multifold out of the depths. Above the nearest mountains, their greens and reds harmonizing with white villages, bluish ridges peered; and beyond, paler and bluer, more and more ridges. Very far away and unreal rose the snow-capped crystalline peaks. Above the acacias and chestnut trees the mighty rocky wall and humpbacked summit of Monte Salute emerged, reddish and light purple. But the people were more beautiful than all the rest. Like flowers they stood in the light beneath the greenery. The emerald parasol glowed like a giant scarab. Ersilia's black hair beneath it, the white slender painter Martha with her rosy face, and all the others. Klingsor drank them in with a thirsty eye, but his thoughts were with Gina. He would not be able to see her for another week. She was sitting in an office in the city, working away at the typewriter; he seldom managed to see her, and never alone. And he loved her, her more than all the others, though she knew nothing about him, did not understand him, regarded him as a strange bird, a famous foreign painter. How strange that was, that his longings should cling to her alone, that no other love sanctified him. It was not like him to go far out of his way for a woman. But he did for Gina, in order to be beside her for an hour, to hold her small slender fingers, to thrust his shoe beneath hers, to imprint a quick kiss on the nape of her neck. He thought about that, a droll puzzle to himself. Was this already the turning point? Old age already coming on? Was it only that, the December–May impulse of the man of forty for the girl of twenty?

They had reached the ridge, and beyond, a new world flung itself at their eyes: Monte Gennaro, high and unreal, piled up out of endless steep, sharp pyramids and cones, the sun aslant behind it, each plateau

glistening enamel floating on deep violet shadows. Between it and themselves the vast areas of shimmering air, and lost in infinite depths the
narrow blue arm of the lake, resting amid the green flames of the
forest.

There was a tiny village on the summit: a smallish manor house,
four or five other houses, of stone, painted blue and pink, a chapel, a
fountain, cherry trees. The company paused by the fountain in the sunlight. Klingsor walked on, through an arched gateway into a shadowy
farmyard. Three bluish buildings stood tall in it, with only a few small
windows, grass and gravel between them, a goat, nettles. A child ran
away from him; he coaxed her to come back, took chocolate from his
pocket. The child stopped; he caught her, caressed her, and pressed the
chocolate upon her. She was shy and lovely, a dark-brown girl with the
alarmed black eyes of a small animal, slender bare legs, brown and
gleaming. 'Where do you live?' he asked her. She ran to the nearest
open door in one of the clifflike houses. From a dark stone room like a
primeval cave a woman stepped, the child's mother; she too accepted
chocolate. Above dirty clothing the brown throat rose, a firm-muscled,
broad face, sun-tanned and beautiful, a broad full mouth, large eyes,
crude sweet charm. Those large, ample Asiatic figures quietly bespoke
sexuality and motherhood. He leaned seductively towards her; smiling,
she held him off, drawing the child between them. He walked on, re-
solved to return. He wanted to paint this woman, or be her lover, if only
for an hour. She was everything: mother, child, mistress, animal,
madonna.

Slowly, he returned to the group, his heart full of dreams. On the
wall of the estate, whose house seemed empty and locked, crude old
cannonballs had been affixed. A whimsical stairway led through shrubbery to a grove and hill with a monument atop it. There, baroque and
solitary, stood a bust: Wallenstein costume, curls, tapering wavy beard.
Ghosts and phantasms shimmered around the mountain in the glaring
midday light. Strange things lurked; the world was tuned to another,
remote key. Klingsor drank at the fountain. A swallowtail butterfly flew
close and sucked at the sprinkled drops on the limestone rim of the
fountain.

The mountain road led along the ridge under chestnuts and walnuts,
in sun and shade. At a bend there was a wayside chapel, old and yellow,
faded old pictures in the niche, a saint's head, angelically sweet and
childlike, a patch of her red and brown garment, the rest crumbled
away. Klingsor loved old pictures, especially when they came his way

unlooked for; he loved such frescoes; he loved the way these beautiful works returned to dust and the earth.

More trees, vines, dazzling hot road. Another turn: there was their destination, suddenly, unexpectedly: a dark arched gateway, a large tall church of red stone, crashing with self-assurance against the sky, a plaza full of sunlight, dust and peace, grass parched to redness, crackling underfoot, noonday light reflected by glaring walls, a column, a figure atop it, invisible in the blaze of sunlight, a stone balustrade around the broad plaza poised over an infinity of blue. Beyond, the village of Kareno, ancient, narrow, densely dark, Saracen, gloomy stone caves under faded brown brick, lanes oppressively narrow as in a dream and full of darkness, small squares suddenly shrieking aloud in white sunlight, Africa and Nagasaki, above the forest, below the blue abyss, higher still the white, plump, saturated clouds.

'It's funny how much time we need before we know our way around in the world just a little,' Klingsor said. 'Once when I was going to Africa, years ago, I passed by this place in an express train, three or five or six miles away, and knew nothing about it. From Africa I went on to Asia, and at the time it was terribly necessary that I do so. But everything I found there I am finding here today: primeval forest, heat, beautiful alien people without nerves, sunlight, temples. It takes so long to learn to visit three continents in a single day. Here they are. Welcome, India! Welcome, Africa! Welcome, Japan!'

The friends knew a young lady who lived up here, and Klingsor was greatly looking forward to meeting the unknown woman. He called her the Queen of the Mountains; that was the title of a mysterious Oriental story in the books of his boyhood.

Expectantly, the caravan penetrated the blue-shaded gorge of the lanes. Not a person, not a sound, not a chicken, not a dog. But in the semishade of a window embrasure Klingsor saw a silent figure standing, a lovely girl, black-eyed, red kerchief around her black hair. Her gaze, lying in wait to capture the stranger, struck his. For the span of a long breath they looked fully, gravely into each other's eyes, two alien worlds momentarily close. Then both smiled briefly, the heartfelt eternal greeting of the sexes, the old, sweet, devouring enmity, and with a step around the corner of the house the stranger had fled away and been placed in the girl's hope chest, a picture among many pictures, a dream among many dreams. The small thorn pricked Klingsor's never-satiated heart; for a moment he hesitated and thought to turn back. Agosto called him; Ersilia began to sing; a shadowy wall vanished and a small, brilliant square with two yellow palazzi lay still and dazzling in the enchanted noon: narrow stone balconies, closed shutters, a glorious stage for the first act of an opera.

'Arrival in Damascus,' the doctor called out. 'Where does Fatima live, the pearl among women?'

The answer came, surprisingly, from the smaller palazzo. Out of the cool blackness behind the half-closed balcony door a strange tone sounded, then another, and the same repeated ten times, then the octave ten times – a piano was being tuned, a melodious piano in the middle of Damascus.

This must be it; this was where she lived. But the house seemed to lack an entrance; there was only the yellow wall with two balconies, and above them a bit of painting in the stucco of the gable: blue and red flowers and a parrot. There should have been a painted door here and if you knocked three times and pronounced Open Sesame the painted door would fly open and the wanderer be greeted by aromatic fragrances, with the Queen of the Mountains seated on a high dais, behind veils, slave girls cowering on the steps at her feet and the painted parrot flying screeching to her mistress's shoulder.

They found a tiny door in a side street. A loud bell, a devilish mechanism, clanged angrily. A small staircase, narrow as a ladder, led upwards. Impossible to imagine how the piano had ever been brought into this house. Through the window? Through the roof?

A large black dog came rushing, a small blond lion after him. A burst of noise; the stairs rattled; in the background the piano sang the same tone eleven times. Sweetly soft light poured out of a room coated with a pinkish whitewash. Doors slammed. Where was the parrot?

Suddenly the Queen of the Mountains stood there, a slender lissome flower, body straight and pliant, all in red, burning flames, image of youth. Before Klingsor's eyes a hundred beloved pictures scattered away and the new picture radiantly took their place. He knew at once that he would paint her, not realistically, but the ray within her that had struck him, the poem, the tart lovely tone: Youth, Redness, Blondeness, Amazon. He would look at her for an hour, perhaps several hours. He would see her walking, sitting, laughing, perhaps dancing, perhaps hear her singing. The day was crowned; the day had been given its meaning. Anything else that might come was pure gift, superfluity. It was always this way: an experience never came alone. Its birds always flew ahead, there were always harbingers and omens: the Asiatic maternal animal look in that doorway, the black-haired village beauty in the window, and now this.

For a second the feeling darted through him: 'If only I were ten years younger, ten brief years, this girl could have me, capture me, wind me around her finger. Now, you are too young, little red queen, too young for the old wizard Klingsor! He will admire you, will get to know you by heart; but he will make no pilgrimage to you, climb no ladder to you, commit no murder for you, and sing no serenades outside your pretty balcony. No, unfortunately he will do none of these things, not the old painter Klingsor, the old ram. He will not love you, he will not cast his eyes at you as he cast his eyes at the Asiatic, at the black-haired girl in the window, who is perhaps not a day younger than you are. He is not too old for her, only for you. Queen of the Mountains, red flower on the hill. For you, wild pink, he is too old. For you the love that Klingsor has to give away between a day full of work and a night full of red wine is not enough. All the better, then, my eye will drink you down, slender rocket, and know you when you have long since faded within me.'

Through stone-floored rooms separated by doorless arches they entered a hall where fantastic baroque plaster figures pranced above tall doors and all around ran a dark frieze of painted dolphins, white horses, and pink Cupids floating in a densely populated mythical sea. There were a few chairs and parts of the disassembled grand piano on the floor, nothing else in the large room. But two alluring doors led to two small balconies above the sun-struck operatic plaza, and diagonally across the balconies of the neighbouring palazzo thrust out, they too wreathed with paintings. There a fat red cardinal floated like a goldfish in the sun.

They stayed. In the big hall provisions were unpacked, a table set. Wine was brought, rare white wine from the north, the key to hosts of memories. The piano tuner had decamped; the dismantled piano held its peace. Thoughtfully, Klingsor stared at the exposed bowels of glittering strings; then he softly closed the lid. His eyes ached, but the summer day sang in his heart, the Saracen mother sang, blue and soaring the dream of Kareno sang. He ate and clinked his glass with the others; he talked gaily in a high voice; and behind it all the apparatus of his workshop operated. His eyes enveloped the wild pink, the field poppy, like water round a fish. A diligent chronicler sat in his brain and carefully wrote down forms, rhythms, movements as if inscribing brazen columns of figures.

Talk and laughter filled the empty room. The doctor's kindly, pru-

dent laugh sounded, Ersilia's low and friendly, Agosto's strong and
subterranean, Martha's birdlike. The poet talked sensibly, Klingsor
jokingly. Watching closely, a little shy, the red queen went among her
guests, dolphins and horses, sped here and there, stood by the piano,
crouched on a cushion, cut bread, poured wine with an inexperienced
girlish hand. Joyousness resounded in the cool hall; eyes glistened dark
and blue; outside the high balcony doors the dazzling noon stared down,
on guard.

The clear, splendid wine flowed into the glasses, delicious contrast
to the simple cold meal. The red glow flowed clear from the queen's
dress through the high room; alert and clear, the eyes of all the men
followed it. She vanished, returned, and had tied on a green sash. She
vanished, returned, and had donned a blue kerchief.

After eating, tired and satiated, they set out gaily for the woods, lay
down in grass and moss. Parasols gleamed, faces glowed under straw
hats, the sun glittered and burned. The Queen of the Mountains lay
redly in the green grass, her fine throat rising white from the flame, her
high shoe intensely coloured and alive on her slender foot. Klingsor,
close by her, read her, studied her, filled himself with her, just as he had
as a boy read the magical story of the Queen of the Mountains and filled
himself with it. They rested, dozed, chattered, flicked at ants, thought
they heard snakes. Prickly chestnut shells clung to the women's hair.
They thought of absent friends who had missed this hour – there were
not many. They wished Louis the Cruel were here, Klingsor's friend,
the painter of carousels and circuses. His antic spirit hovered above the
group, close by.

The afternoon passed like a year in paradise. There was a great deal
of laughter when they parted from the Queen. Klingsor took everything
with him in his heart: the Queen, the woods, the palazzo and the dol-
phin room, the two dogs, the parrot.

Descending the mountain among his friends, there gradually came
over him that exuberant mood that he had only on rare days when he
had voluntarily let his work go. Hand in hand with Ersilia, with Hermann, with Martha, he danced down the sunlit road, starting songs,
taking childlike pleasure in jokes and puns, surrendering to laughter.
He ran ahead of the others and lay in ambush to frighten them.

Quickly as they walked, the sun sank more quickly. By the time they
reached Palazzetto it had dropped behind the mountain, and in the
valley below, it was already evening. They had missed the way and
descended too low; they were hungry and tired and had to abandon

their plans for the evening: a stroll through the fields to Barengo, a fish dinner in the lakeside village's restaurant.

'My dears,' Klingsor said, sitting down on a wall by the wayside, 'our plans were all very fine, and I would certainly be grateful for a good dinner among the fishermen or in Monte d'Oro. But we cannot make it that far, or at least I cannot. I'm tired and I'm hungry. I'm not taking another step beyond the nearest grotto, which certainly isn't far. There we can get bread and wine. That's enough. Who's coming?'

They all came. They found the grotto; on a narrow terrace cut into the forested hill stood stone benches and tables under the darkness of trees. From the wine cellar in the cavern the innkeeper brought cool wine. There was bread on the tables. Now they sat eating in silence, glad to be sitting down at last. Beyond the tall tree trunks the day faded out; the blue mountain turned black, the red road white. Down below, on the nocturnal road, they could hear a car, and a dog barking. Here and there stars appeared in the sky, and in the landscape below lights winked on; there was no telling the two apart.

Klingsor sat happily resting, looking out into the night, slowly checking his hunger with black bread, quietly draining the bluish cups of wine. Satiated, he began to talk again and to sing; he rocked to the beat of the songs, played with the women, sniffed the fragrance of their hair. The wine seemed good to him. Practiced seducer, he easily talked down the proposals that they go on their way. He drank wine, poured wine, sent for more wine. Slowly, out of the bluish earthenware cups, symbol of transitoriness, bright spells arose, magic transforming the world, colouring the stars and lights.

They sat in a swing hovering high above the abyss of world and night, birds in a golden cage, homeless, weightless, across from the stars. They sang, these birds, sang exotic songs; out of ecstatic hearts they cast fantasies into the night, into the sky, into the woods, into the enchanted universe. Answers came from stars and moon, from trees and mountains. Goethe sat there and his alter ego Hafis; torrid Egypt and grave Greece rose up; Mozart smiled; Hugo Wolf played the piano in the delirious night.

There was a crash of noise, a blaze of light; below them, straight through the heart of the earth, with a hundred dazzling lighted windows, a railroad train streaked into the mountain and into the night. In the sky above, the bells of an invisible church rang. With a skulking air the half moon rose above the table, glanced at its reflection in the dark wine, marked a woman's mouth and eye off from the darkness, mounted higher, sang to the stars. The spirit of Louis the Cruel sat hunched, solitary, on a bench, writing letters.

Klingsor, King of the Night, tall crown in his hair, leaning back on his throne of stone, directed the dance of the world, set the beat, called forth the moon, willed that the railroad train vanish. At once it was gone, as a constellation plummets over the margin of the sky. Where was the Queen of the Mountains? Was that not a piano sounding in the woods? Was not the mistrustful little lion barking far off? Had she not been wearing a blue kerchief a moment ago? Hello, old world, see to it that you don't collapse! Come here, woods! Go there, black mountain! Keep to the beat! Stars, how blue and red you are, as in the folk song: 'Your red eyes and your blue mouth!'

Painting was lovely; painting was a dear, lovely game for well-behaved children. But it was something else, grander and more momentous, to direct the movements of the stars, to project the beat of your own blood, the circlets of colour from your own retina, into the world, to send the vibrations of your own soul thrumming out with the wind of the night. Away with you, black mountains! Become a cloud, fly to Persia, rain on Uganda! Come here, spirit of Shakespeare, sing us your drunken fool's song of the rain that raineth every day!

Klingsor kissed a woman's small hand, leaned against a woman's sweetly rising and falling breast. A foot under the table played with his. He did not know whose hand or whose foot; he felt tenderness all around him, gratefully felt old magic renewed. He was still young, it was still far from the end, he was still capable of radiation and allure; they still loved him, the good anxious little females, they still counted on him.

He soared higher. In a low, chanting voice he began to tell a tale, a tremendous epic, the story of a love affair, or rather it was really a trip to the South Seas where in the company of Gauguin and Crusoe he discovered Parrot Island and founded the Free State of the Blessed Isles. How the thousands of parrots had sparkled in the twilight, how their blue tails had glittered, mirrored in the green bay! Their cries, and the hundred-voiced shrieks of the big monkeys, had greeted him like thunder – him, Klingsor, when he proclaimed his Free State. He had called upon the white cockatoo to form a cabinet, and with the sulky rhinoceros bird he had drunk palm wine from heavy coconut cups. O moon of the past, moon of the blissful nights, moon above the pile dwelling among the reeds! The shy brown princess bore the name of Kül Kalüa; slender and long-limbed she strode through the banana forest, gleaming like honey under the succulent roof of the giant leaves, doe-eyed, cat-backed, feline tension in springy ankle and sinewy leg. Kül Kalüa, child, archaic ardour and childish innocence of the sacred southeast; for a thousand nights you lay upon Klingsor's heart and every night was new, each was sweeter, each tenderer than all the others. O festival of the Earth Spirit when the virgins of the Parrot Islands dance before the god!

Over the islands, over Crusoe and Klingsor, over the tale and the listeners, the white-starred night arched, the mountain swelled like gently breathing belly and breasts under the trees and houses and the feet of men; the racing moon danced feverishly over the firmament, pursued by the stars in wild and silent choreography. Strings of stars lined up, the glittering wire of a cable railway to Paradise. Primeval forest darkened maternally, primordial mud wafted the scent of decay and generation, serpents and crocodiles crawled, the stream of forms poured on without bounds or banks.

'I'm going to paint again after all,' Klingsor said. 'I'll start again tomorrow. But no more of these houses and people and trees. I'll paint crocodiles and starfish, dragons and purple snakes, and everything that is changing, filled with longing to become man, full of longing to become stars, full of birth, full of decay, full of God and death.'

In the midst of his almost whispered words, in the midst of the wild drunken hour, Ersilia's voice sounded low and clear. Quietly she sang the song of *bel mazzo di fiori* under her breath. Tranquillity poured from her song; Klingsor heard it as if it came from some distant floating island across seas of time and solitude. He turned his empty wine cup over, filled it no more. He listened. A child sang. A mother sang. What was he – an errant and reprobate fellow bathed in the mire of the world, a scoundrel and profligate, or was he a silly small child?

'Ersilia,' he said with reverence, 'you are our lucky star.'

Up the mountain through the steep dark woods, clinging to branches and roots, they sought their homeward path, reached the margin of the woods, boarded a field like pirates on a ship. The narrow path through the cornfield breathed night and homecoming, moon glancing against the shiny leaves of corn, rows of grapevines slanting away. Now Klingsor sang, softly, in his somewhat hoarse voice, sang many murmuring songs, German and Malay, with and without words. Singing low he poured out all that had accumulated within him, as a brown wall at evening radiates the stored daylight.

Here one of the friends took his leave, another there, vanishing along narrow paths in the shadow of the grapes. Each left, each went by himself, heading home, alone under the sky. A woman kissed Klingsor good night; burning, her mouth sipped at his. They rolled away, they melted away, all of them. When Klingsor, alone, climbed the stairs to his dwelling, he was still singing. He sang the praises of God and himself; he praised Li Po and the good wine of Pampambio. Like an idol, he rested upon clouds of affirmation.

'Inwardly,' he sang, 'I am like a ball of gold, like the dome of a cathedral; people kneel in it, people pray, gold gleams from the wall, the Saviour bleeds in an old painting, the heart of Mary bleeds. We bleed too, we others, we errant souls, we stars and comets; seven and fourteen swords pierce our blessed chests. I love you, blonde and dark women, I love all, even the philistines; you are all poor devils like myself, all poor children and misbegotten demigods like drunken Klingsor. Beloved life, I greet you! I greet you, beloved death!'

Klingsor to Edith

Dear Star in the Summer Sky,

How well and truly you have written to me, and how painfully your love calls to me, like eternal song, like eternal reproach. For you are on a good course when you confess to me, when you confess to yourself, every stirring of the heart. But do not call any emotion petty, any emotion unworthy. Every one is good, very good, even hatred, even envy, even jealousy, even cruelty. All we live on are our poor, lovely, glorious feelings, and each one we wrong is a star we have extinguished.

I don't know whether I love Gina. I doubt it very much. I would not make any sacrifices for her. I do not know whether I can love at all. I can desire and can seek myself in others; I can listen for an echo, demand a mirror, seek pleasure, and all that can look like love.

Both of us, you and I, are wandering in the same maze, in the maze of our feelings, which have been scanted in this sorry world, for which reason we take revenge on this evil world, each in his own fashion. But let us, each of us, let the other's dreams remain, because we know how sweet and red the wine of dreams tastes.

Clarity about their feelings and about the 'importance' and consequences of their actions is something that only good, self-assured people have, those who believe in life and take no step that they will not be able to approve tomorrow and the day after as well. I am not lucky enough to be one of them, and I feel and act like a man who does not believe in tomorrow and regards every day as his last.

Dear Sylph, I am unlucky in my efforts to express my thoughts.

Expressed thoughts are always so dead. Let us allow them to live! I feel deeply and gratefully that you understand me, that something in you is akin to me. I don't know under what heading that should be placed in the book of life, whether our feelings are love, sex, gratitude, or sympathy, whether they are maternal or childish. Often I look at every woman like a cunning old libertine, and often like a little boy. Often the chastest woman tempts me most, and often the lushest. Everything I am permitted to love is beautiful, holy, infinitely good. But why, how long, to what degree I may love – that I cannot judge.

I do not love you alone, as you well know, nor do I love Gina alone. Tomorrow and the day after tomorrow I shall love other women, paint other pictures. But I shall not regret any love I have ever felt, and any wise or foolish act that I have committed for those loves' sakes. Perhaps I love you because you are like me. I love others because they are so different from me.

It is late in the night; the moon stands over Salute. How life smiles, how death smiles!

Throw this silly letter into the fire, and throw into the fire

Your Klingsor

The Music of Doom

The last day of July had come, Klingsor's favourite month; Li Po's grand festival had faded, had not been repeated. Sunflowers in the garden brashly raised their gold to the blue. Together with his faithful Tu Fu, Klingsor tramped through a region that he loved: the parched outskirts of a town, dusty roads beneath high rows of trees, red and orange little houses facing the sandy shore, trucks and quays, long violet walls, colourful poor folk. In the evening he sat in the dust at the edge of the town and painted the coloured tents and wagons of an itinerant carnival; he crouched by the side of the road on scruffy, parched greensward, beguiled by the strong colours of the tents. He clung fast to the faded lilac of a tent tassel, to the jolly greens and reds of the clumsy trailer homes, to the blue-and-white framing poles. Fiercely, he wallowed in cadmium, savagely in cool sweet cobalt, drew melting lines of crimson lake through the yellow and green sky. Another hour, no, less, then he would knock off, night would come, and tomorrow August would be starting, August the burning fever month which mixes so much fear of death and timorousness into its ardent cup. The scythe was sharpened, the day declined; death laughed, concealed among the parching leaves. Ring high and blast your trumpet, cadmium! Boast loudly, lush crimson lake! Laugh glaringly, lemon yellow! Come here, you deep-blue mountain in the distance. Come to my heart, you matt dusty green trees. How tired you are, how you let your pious branches droop submissively. I drink to you, lovely things of the world! I give you semblance of duration and immortality, I who am the most transitory, the most believing, the saddest of all, who suffer from the fear of death more than all of you. July is burned out, soon August will be burned out; suddenly the great ghost chills us from the yellowed leaves in the dew-wet morning. Suddenly November sweeps across the woods. Suddenly the great ghost laughs, suddenly the chill settles around our hearts, suddenly the dear pink flesh falls from our bones, the jackal howls in the desert, the vulture hoarsely sings his accursed song. An accursed news-paper in the city publishes my picture, and under it the words: 'Out-standing painter, expressionist, great colourist, died on the sixteenth of this month.'

Full of hatred he ripped a furrow of Paris blue under the green gypsy wagon. Full of bitterness, he broke the chrome-yellow edge of the curb-stones. Full of deep despair, he dashed vermilion in an empty spot, annihilating the challenging white; bleeding, he fought for continuance. He screamed in bright green and Neapolitan yellow to inexorable God. Groaning, he threw more blue into the dreary dusty green; imploringly, he kindled deeper lights in the evening sky. The little palette full of pure unmixed colours, intensely luminous, was his comfort, his tower, his arsenal, his prayer book, his cannon. From it he fired upon wicked death. Purple was denial of death, vermilion was mockery of decay. His arsenal was good; his brave troop stood lined up brilliantly, the rapid rounds from his cannon flashed. But it was no use, all shooting was in vain; and yet shooting was good, was happiness and consolation, was still living, still triumphing.

Tu Fu had left to visit a friend who had his magic citadel over there between the factory and the wharf. Now he returned, bringing with him the Armenian astrologer.

Klingsor, finished with the painting, drew a deep breath of relief when he saw the two faces close by, the good fair hair of Tu Fu and the black beard with white teeth in the smiling face of the magus. With them came the shadow also, the long dark shadow with receding eyes in deep sockets. Welcome, you too, Shadow, fine fellow!

'Do you know what day today is?' Klingsor asked his friend.

'The last day of July, I know.'

'I cast a horoscope today,' the Armenian said, 'and I saw that this evening is going to bring me something. Saturn stands strangely, Mars neutral, Jupiter is dominant. Li Po, aren't you a Leo?'

'I was born on July the second.'

'I thought so. Your stars stand confusedly, Friend; only you yourself can interpret them. Fertility surrounds you like a cloud about to burst. Your stars stand oddly, Klingsor; I'm sure you can't help feeling it.'

Klingsor packed up his gear. The world he had painted was faded, the green and yellow sky extinguished, the bright blue flag drowned, the lovely yellow slain and withered. He was hungry and thirsty; his throat felt full of dust.

'Friends,' he said cordially, 'let us spend this evening together. We shall no longer be together again, all four of us; I am not reading that in the stars, but I find it written in my heart. My July moon is over; its last hours glow darkly; in the depths the Great Mother calls. Never has the world been so beautiful, never have I painted so beautiful a picture. Heat lightning flashes; the music of doom has begun. Let us sing along with it, the sweet forbidding music. Let us stay together and drink wine and eat bread.'

Beside the carousel, whose tent had just been taken down in preparation for the evening (for it was there as a sunshade), a few tables stood under the trees. A lame waitress was going back and forth; there was a small tavern in the shade. Here they sat at the plank table; bread was brought, and wine poured into the earthenware vessels. Lights glowed into life under the trees. A short distance away the carousel's hurdy-gurdy began to jingle, loosing its shrill music into the evening.

'I mean to drain three hundred cups tonight!' Li Po cried, and toasted the Shadow. 'Greetings, Shadow, steadfast tin soldier! Greetings, friends! Greetings, electric lights, arc lamps and sparkling merry-go-round spangles! Oh, if only Louis were here, the fugitive bird! Perhaps he's already flown on ahead of us to heaven. Or perhaps he'll come back tomorrow, the old jackal, and no longer find us and laugh and plant arc lamps and flagpoles upon our grave.'

Quietly, the astrologer went and returned with fresh wine, his white teeth smiling gladly in his red mouth.

'Melancholia,' he said with a glance at Klingsor, 'is a thing we should not carry around. It's so easy – it's the work of an hour, a single intensive hour with clenched teeth, and then one is through with melancholia forever.'

Klingsor looked closely at his mouth, at the bright, straight teeth that had once upon a time, in some fervid hour, crunched melancholia and bitten it to death. Could he too do what the astrologer had succeeded in doing? O sweet brief glance into distant gardens: life without dread, life without melancholia! But he knew these gardens were unattainable for him. He knew his destiny was different, Saturn lowered differently upon him, God wanted him to play different tunes upon his strings.

'Each has his stars,' Klingsor said slowly. 'Each has his faith. I believe in only one thing: in doom. We are driving in a carriage on the edge of an abyss, and the horses have already shied. We are immersed in doom, all of us; we must die, we must be born again. The great turning point has come for us. It is the same everywhere: the great war, the great change in art, the great collapse in the governments of the West. For us in old Europe everything we had that was good and our own has already died. Our fine-feathered Reason has become madness, our money is paper, our machines can do nothing but shoot and explode, our art is suicide. We are going under, friends; that is our destiny. Music in the Tsing Tse key has begun.'

The Armenian poured wine.

'As you like,' he said. 'One can say yes and one can say no; that is only a child's game. Doom is something that does not exist. For doom or resurgence to exist there must be a top and a bottom. But there is no top or bottom; these exist only in man's brain, which is the home of illusion. All paradoxes are illusions: white and black are illusion, death and life are illusion, good and evil are illusion. It is the work of an hour, a single fervent hour with clenched teeth, and one has overcome the kingdom of illusions.'

Klingsor listened to his good voice.

'I am speaking of us,' he retorted. 'I am speaking of Europe, our old Europe that for two thousand years thought itself the world's brain. It is going under. Do you think, Magus, that I don't know you? You are a messenger from the East, a messenger to me also, perhaps a spy, perhaps a warlord in disguise. You are here because the end is beginning, because the scent of doom is in your nostrils. But we are glad to go under, you know, we die gladly, we do not defend ourselves.'

'You may also say: we are glad to be born,' the Asiatic said, laughing. 'To you it seems doom, perhaps to me it seems birth. Both are illusion. The man who believes in the earth as a fixed disk under heaven also sees and believes in sunrise and sunset, in dawn and doom – and all, almost all men believe in that fixed disk! The stars themselves know nothing of rising and setting.'

'Have not the stars set, are not the stars doomed too?' Tu Fu cried.

'For us, for our eyes.'

He filled the cups; it was always he who undertook to pour, attentively, smilingly. He went away with the empty pitcher to bring more wine. The carousel music blared.

'Let's go over there, it's so lovely,' Tu Fu pleaded, and they went over to the carousel, stood by the painted barrier, watched the carousel turn its giddy circles in the piercing glitter of spangles and mirrors. They saw a hundred children with eyes greedily fixed on the brilliance. For a moment Klingsor felt, with deep amusement, the primitiveness and African quality of this whirling machine, this mechanical music, these garish pictures and colours, mirrors and insane ornamental columns. Everything bespoke medicine men and shamans, magic and age-old pied-piperism, and all that wild weird sparkle was at bottom nothing but the darting glitter of the tin lure that the pike thinks is a minnow.

Every child must ride the carousel. Tu Fu gave money to the children; the Shadow beckoned to all the children to come nearer. They clustered around their benefactor, clung to him, begged, thanked. There was a pretty blonde girl of twelve who asked repeatedly; she rode on every round. In the glitter of the lights her short skirt blew up around her boyish legs. One child cried. Boys fought. The cymbals clanged sharply along with the organ, poured fire into the beat, opium into the wine. For a long while the four stood amid the tumult.

Then they returned to their quiet table under the trees. The Armenian filled the cups with wine, stirred up doom, smiled brightly.

'Let us empty three hundred cups today,' Klingsor sang. His sunbleached hair glowed yellow, his laughter boomed. Melancholia knelt, a giant, upon his twitching heart. He held up his glass in a toast, he hailed doom, hailed the desire for death, the Tsing Tse key. The carousel music surged and roared. But inside his heart, dread lurked. The heart did not want to die. The heart hated death.

Suddenly more music assaulted the night, shrill, intemperate, from the tavern. In the nook beside the chimney piece, whose shelf was lined with neatly arranged wine bottles, a player-piano blazed, machinegun fire, wild, hectoring, impetuous. Sorrow cried from discordant strings, steam-roller rhythm flattened groaning dissonances. There was a crowd here too, light, noise, young men and girls dancing, the lame waitress too, and Tu Fu. He danced with the blonde little girl. Klingsor watched. Lightly, sweetly, her short summer dress whirled around the pretty skinny legs. Tu Fu's face smiled amiably, filled with love. The others sat at the chimney piece; they had come in from the garden, were close to the source of the music, in the very midst of it. Klingsor saw tones, heard colours. The magus took one and another bottle from the shelf, opened them, poured. His smile never wavered on his brown intelligent face. The music thumped fearfully in the low-ceilinged hall. Slowly the Armenian opened a breach in the row of old bottles on the mantle, like a temple robber removing, chalice by chalice, the precious utensils from an altar.

'You are a great artist,' the astrologer whispered to Klingsor as he filled his cup. 'You are one of the greatest artists of this age. You are quite entitled to call yourself Li Po. But, Li Po, you are a poor, harried, tormented, and anxiety-ridden man. You have struck up the music of doom; you sit singing in your burning house, which you yourself have set afire, and you do not feel happy about it, Li Po, even if you empty three hundred cups every day and drink with the moon. You are not happy about it, you are very sorry about it, singer of doom. Won't you stop? Don't you want to live? Don't you want to continue?'

Klingsor drank and whispered back in his somewhat hoarse voice: 'Can a man change fate? Is there freedom of the will? Can you, astrologer, guide my stars differently?'

'I cannot guide them, only interpret them. Only you yourself can guide. There is freedom of the will. It is the wisdom of the Magi.'

'Why should I practise the wisdom of the Magi when I can practise art? Isn't art just as good?'

'Everything is good. Nothing is good. The wisdom of the Magi abolishes illusions. It abolishes that worst of illusions which we call "time."'

'Doesn't art do that also?'

'It tries to. Is your painted July, which you have there in your portfolio, enough for you? Have you abolished time? Are you without fear of the autumn, of the winter?'

Klingsor sighed and fell silent. Silently, he drank. Silently, the magus filled his cup. Hectically, the unleashed mechanical piano rumbled. Angelically, Tu Fu's face floated among the dancers. July was over.

Klingsor toyed with the empty bottles on the table, arranging them in a circle.

'These are our cannon,' he exclaimed. 'With these cannon we shoot time to pieces, death to pieces, misery to pieces. I have also shot at death with paints, with fiery green and explosive vermilion and sweet scarlet lake. Often I have hit him on the head; I have driven white and blue into his eye. I have often sent him scurrying. I shall meet him often again, overcome him, outwit him. Look at the Armenian; he is opening another old bottle and the imprisoned sun of past summers shoots into our blood. The Armenian, too, helps us shoot at death; the Armenian, too, knows no other weapon against death.'

The magus broke bread and ate.

'I need no weapon against death because there is no death. There is only one thing: dread of death. That can be cured; there is a weapon to use against that. It is a matter of an hour to overcome that dread. But Li Po does not want to. For Li loves death; he loves his dread of death, his melancholy, his misery. Only his dread has taught him all that he can do and all we love him for.'

Mockingly, he raised his cup to Klingsor's; his teeth flashed, his face grew more and more jovial. Sorrow seemed alien to him. No one answered. Klingsor shot his wine cannon against death. Death loomed at the open doors of the tavern, which was swollen with people, wine, and dance music. Death loomed at the doors, softly shook the black acacia, lurked darkly in the garden. Everything outside was full of death, filled with death; only here in the crowded hall they still fought on, fought gloriously and bravely against the black besieger who whimpered at the windows.

Mockingly, the magus looked across the table; mockingly, he filled the cups. Klingsor had already broken many cups; the magus had given him new ones. The Armenian had also drunk a great many, but he sat as erect as Klingsor.

'Let us drink, Li,' he said in low-voiced mockery. 'You love death, you know, you want to be doomed, you are glad to die the death. Didn't you say so, or have I deceived myself – or have you after all deceived me and yourself? Let us drink, Li, let us be doomed.'

Rage bubbled up in Klingsor. He stood up, stood erect and tall, the old sparrow-hawk with his chiselled face, spat into the wine, hurled his full cup on the floor. The red wine splashed out into the hall; his friends paled, strangers laughed.

But smiling silently the magus fetched a new cup, smilingly filled it, smilingly offered it to Li Po. Then Li smiled, he too smiled. A smile flickered like moonlight over his distorted face.

'Friends,' he cried out, 'let this foreigner talk! The old fox knows a great deal; he has come out of a deep and hidden den. He knows a great deal, but he does not understand us. He is too old to understand children. He is too wise to understand fools. We who are about to die know more about death than he. We are men, not stars. See my hand, holding a small blue cup of wine! This hand, this brown hand, can do many things. It has painted with many brushes, has wrested fresh segments of the world from the darkness and placed them before men's eyes. This brown hand has stroked many women under the chin and seduced many girls. Many have kissed it, tears have fallen on it, Tu Fu has written a poem to it. This dear hand, friends, will soon be full of earth and maggots; none of you would touch it then. Very well, that is the reason I love it. I love my hand, I love my eyes, I love my soft white belly; I love them with regret and with scorn and with great tenderness because they must all wither and decay so soon. Shadow, dark friend, old tin soldier on Andersen's grave, you too will meet the same fate, dear fellow. Drink with me: Three cheers for our limbs and guts! Long may they live!'

They drank the toast. The Shadow smiled darkly from his deep eye sockets – and suddenly something passed through the hall like a wind, like a spirit. Abruptly the music stopped, the dancers vanished, as if swallowed by the night, and half the lights went out. Klingsor looked at the black doors. Outside stood death. He saw death standing there. He smelled him. Like raindrops in the leaves by the highroad, that was how death smelled.

Then Li Po pushed the cup away, knocked back the chair, and walked slowly out of the hall into the dark garden and on, in the darkness, heat lightning flashing over his head, alone. His heart lay heavy in his breast like the stone upon a grave.

Evening in August

Klingsor had spent the afternoon at Manuzzo and Veglia, painting in sun and wind. In the gathering twilight he had crossed over Veglia, very tired, to a small, sleeping village. He succeeded in routing out a grey-haired innkeeper's wife; she brought him wine. He sat down on the stump of a walnut tree outside the door, unpacked his knapsack, found a piece of cheese and a few plums still left, and had his supper. The old woman sat by, stooped and toothless, and with wrinkled throat working and quiescent old eyes spoke of the life of her hamlet and her family, of the war and the rising prices, and of the state of the fields, of wine and milk and what they cost, of dead grandchildren and emigrant sons. All the constellations and seasons of the farm woman's life lay spread out before Klingsor, clearly, pleasingly, coarsely in their sparse beauty, full of gladnesses and concerns, full of anxiety and life. Klingsor ate, drank, rested, listened, asked about children and livestock, priest and bishop, amiably praised the wretched wine, offered a last plum to her, shook hands, wished her a happy night, and leaning on his stick, laden with his knapsack, climbed slowly up the mountain through the thin woods to his bed for the night.

It was that glorious hour, with the daylight still glowing everywhere but the moon already gleaming and the first bats dipping in the green, shimmering air. One edge of woods stood dissolving in the last light, bright chestnut trunks against black shadows. A yellow cottage softly radiated the daylight it had absorbed, glowing gently like a topaz. The small paths, pink and violet, led through meadows, vineyards, and woods. Here and there an acacia twig had already yellowed. The western sky hung golden and green above the velvet blue mountains.

Oh, to be able to work now, in this last enchanted quarter hour of the ripe summer's day which would never come again! How inexpressibly beautiful everything was now, how peaceful, good, and giving, as if filled with God.

Klingsor sat down in the cool grass, mechanically reached for his pencil, then smilingly let his hand drop again. He was dead tired. He fingered the dry grass, the dry crumbly earth. How much longer, and then this wonderful game was over! How much longer, and then hand and mouth and eyes would be full of earth! A few days ago Tu Fu had sent him a poem. He remembered it now and spoke it slowly under his breath:

Leaf after leaf descends
From my life's tree.
O world's magnificence
How you fill me,
How you fill and satiate,
How you inebriate.
What burns today
Is soon decay.
Soon the wind keens
Over my brown grave.
The mother leans
Over the child's face.
Let me see her eyes again,
My star is in her eyes.
Nothing else need remain,
All that dies gladly dies.
Only the eternal Mother stays
From whom we came,
Lightly her finger plays,
Inscribes in air: our name.

Well, it was good that it was so. How many of his ten lives did Klingsor have left? Three? Two? It was still more than one, still more than one respectable, ordinary, everyday, commonplace life. And how much he had seen, how much paper and canvas he had covered, how many hearts he had stirred in love and hate, in art and life, how much vexation and fresh wind he had brought into the world. He had loved many women, destroyed many traditions and sanctuaries, dared many new things. He had emptied many full cups, breathed in many days and starry nights, grown tanned under many suns, swum in many waters. Now he sat here, in Italy or India or China; the summer wind puffed whimsically at the crowns of the chestnuts, the world was good, was perfect. It did not matter whether he painted another hundred pictures or ten, or whether he lived another twenty summers or one. He was tired, tired. All that dies gladly dies. Dear, good Tu Fu!

It was time to go home. He would totter into the room, be received by the breeze through the balcony door. He would strike a light and unpack. The heart of the woods with all that chrome yellow and chinese blue might be good; it would make a picture some day. Get going then, it was time.

Nevertheless, he stayed where he was, the wind in his hair, sitting in his flapping, paint-stained linen jacket, a smile and a grief in his twilight heart. Softly, slackly, the wind blew, softly, silently, the bats dipped against the fading sky. All that dies gladly dies. Only the eternal Mother stays.

He might sleep here, at least for an hour. It was warm, after all. He pillowed his head on his knapsack and looked up into the sky. How beautiful the world is, how it satiates.

Footsteps sounded, descending the mountain, walking strongly on loose wooden soles. Between the fern and the broom a figure appeared, a woman; it was already so dark that he could not make out the colours of her dress. She approached closer, with sound, even steps. Klingsor jumped up and called out good evening. She started a little, and paused for a moment. He looked into her face. He knew her but could not remember where he had seen her. She was pretty and dark; her fine, firm teeth flashed. 'Well, well!' he exclaimed, holding out his hand to her. He sensed that something linked him with this woman, some small recollection. 'Don't we know each other?'

'Madonna! Why, you're the painter from Castagnetta. Do you still remember me?'

Yes, now he knew. She was a peasant woman from the Taverne valley. Once upon a time, in the shadowy and confused past of this summer, he had painted near her house for a few hours, had taken water from her well, had napped for an hour in the shade of the fig tree, and at the end received a glass of wine and a kiss from her.

'You never came back,' she complained. 'And you promised so that you would.'

There was wantonness and provocation in her deep voice. Klingsor revived.

'*Ecco*, so much the better that you've come to me now. What luck I have, just now, when I'm so lonely and sad.'

'Sad? Don't try to fool me, *signore*, you're a joker, a woman can't believe a word you say. I must go on now.'

'Oh, then I'll keep you company.'

'This isn't the way you go, and there's no need either. What could happen to me?'

'Not to you, but to me. How easy it would be for some man to come along and strike your fancy and go with you and kiss your sweet mouth and your throat and your beautiful breast, someone else besides me. No, that can't be allowed.'

He had ringed her nape with his hand and would not let her go. 'My little star. Sweetheart. My sweet little plum. Bite me, or I'll eat you.'

He kissed her on her strong, open mouth. Laughing, she bent back; between resisting and protesting she yielded, kissed him back, shook her head, laughed, tried to free herself. He held her tightly, his mouth on hers, his hand on her breast. Her hair smelled like summer, like hay, broom, fern, brambles. Taking a deep breath, for a moment he bent his head back and saw, small and white in the faded sky, the first star rising. The woman spoke no more; her face had become grave. She sighed, placed her hand on his and pressed it more firmly against her breast. He stooped gently, pressed his arm into the unresisting hollows of her knees, and bedded her down in the grass.

'Do you like me?' she asked like a little girl. '*Povera me!*'

They drank the cup. Wind brushed over their hair and carried their breath with it.

Before they parted he looked in his knapsack and his coat pockets to see if he had anything to give her. He found a small silver case, still half full of cigarette tobacco. He emptied it and gave it to her.

'No, not a present, certainly not!' he assured her. 'Only a memento, so you won't forget me.'

'I won't forget you,' she said. And, 'Will you come again?'

He became sad. Slowly he kissed her on both eyes. 'I'll come again,' he said.

For a while he stood motionless, listening to her wooden clogs clacking downhill, over the meadow at the bottom, through the woods, clacking on earth, on rock, on leaves, on roots. Now she was gone. The woods stood black against the night, the wind brushed warmly over the invisible earth. Something, perhaps a mushroom, perhaps a withered fern, smelled acridly of autumn.

Klingsor could not make up his mind to go home. What was the point of climbing the mountain now, of going into the room with all the pictures? He stretched out in the grass and looked at the stars. At last he slept, and slept until late in the night the cry of an animal or a gust of wind or the coolness of the dew roused him. Then he climbed up to Castagnetta, found his house, his door, his room. Letters lay there, and flowers; friends had dropped by.

Tired as he was, he obeyed the tenacious old habit of every night, unpacking all his things and looking at the day's sketches by lamplight. That one of the depths of the woods was good; the plants and rocks in the light-flecked shade gleamed cool and precious like a treasure chamber. It had been a happy thought to have worked only with chrome yellow, orange, and blue and left out the chrome green. For a long while he studied the sheet.

But what for? What were all these sheets smeared with colour for? Why all the toil, all the sweat, all the brief, drunken lust of creativity? Was there redemption? Was there tranquillity? Was there peace?

As soon as he had undressed he sank exhausted into bed, put out the light and sought sleep, softly humming Tu Fu's verses to himself:

> Soon the wind keens
> Over my brown grave.

Klingsor writes to
Louis the Cruel

Caro Luigi, it is long since I have heard your voice. Do you still live in the light? Is the vulture already gnawing your bones?

Have you ever used a darning needle to poke at a stopped clock? I did so once, and suddenly the devil got into the works and rattled off all the time that had passed; the hands raced each other around the face, whirling madly away with an uncanny noise, *prestissimo*, until suddenly everything snapped and the clock gave up the ghost. It is just like that right now with us here: the sun and moon are running amok across the sky, the days flying by, time running away with me as if pouring out of a hole in a bag. I hope the end will come suddenly and this drunken world will cease instead of dropping back again into a respectable tempo.

All through the days I have been too busy to be able to think of anything (how funny that sounds, by the way, when I say such a so-called 'phrase' aloud to myself: 'to be able to think of anything'). But in the evenings I often miss you. Usually I sit in the forest at one of the many *caves* drinking the popular red wine, which for the most part is of very poor quality but still helps to make life bearable and brings on sleep. Several times I have actually fallen asleep at the table in the grotto, thus proving to the grinning natives that my neurasthenia really cannot be all that bad. Sometimes friends and girls are with me and I practise my fingers on the Plasticine of female limbs and chatter about hats and heels and art. Sometimes we're lucky enough to hit a good temperature; then we shout and laugh all night long and people are glad that Klingsor is such a jolly old fellow. There is a very pretty woman here who asks after you every time I see her, with passionate interest.

The art we both practise still depends, as a professor would say, too much upon the object (how nice it would be to paint a picture puzzle). We are still – though in a somewhat free handwriting and a way that's upsetting enough to the bourgeois – painting the things of 'reality': people, trees, country fairs, railroads, landscapes. In that respect we're still obeying a convention. The bourgeois calls those things 'real' which are seen and described pretty much the same way by everybody, or at least by many people. As soon as this summer is over, I have in mind to paint nothing but fantasies for a while, especially dreams. Some of it will be the way you like it, zany and surprising, something like Collofino the Rabbit Hunter's tales of Cologne Cathedral. Even though I feel that the ground under my feet has somewhat thinned out and even though on the whole I have little craving for more years and more accomplishments, still I'd like to send a few more violent rockets into the maw of this universe. A collector recently wrote me that he was delighted to observe that I was experiencing a second youth in my latest works. There's something to that. It seems to me I've only begun to really paint this year. But what I'm experiencing is not so much a springtime as an explosion. Amazing how much dynamite there's still left in me. But dynamite is hard to burn in one of those ranges that make the most of every stick of wood.

Dear Louis, I'm often amused that we two old libertines are at bottom so touchingly shamefaced and would rather throw our wine glasses at each other's heads than show anything of our feelings. May it remain so, old hedgehog!

Lately we had a grand party on bread and wine at that grotto near Barengo. Our singing echoed gloriously in the tall woods at midnight, the old Roman songs. We need so little for happiness when we grow older and begin freezing down at the feet: eight to ten hours' work a day, a bottle of Piedmontese, a half pound of bread, a cigar, a few girls, and of course warmth and good weather. That we have; the sun is doing its duty splendidly. My head is as tanned as a mummy's.

Some days I have the feeling that my life and work are just beginning, but sometimes it seems to me I've slaved away for eighty years and can soon lay claim to peace and rest. Everybody reaches an end some day, my Louis, and so will I, so will you. God knows what I'm writing you; it's plain that I'm not feeling well. Probably hypochondria; my eyes hurt a great deal, and sometimes a treatise that I read years ago on detachment of the retina preys on my mind.

When I look down from my balcony door, at the view you know, I realize that we have to go on working hard for a good while yet. The world is inexpressibly beautiful and various; it clangs up to me day and night through this high green door, screaming and demanding, and I run out again and again and snatch a piece of it for myself, a tiny piece. The dry summer has done great things to the greenery hereabouts; I never would have thought that I would have to resort to English red and burnt sienna again. And then the whole autumn is waiting, stubble fields, wine harvest, corn harvest, crimson forests. I'll go through all that once more, day after day, and do a few hundred more studies. But then, I feel it, I shall be turning inward and once again, as I did for a while as a young fellow, paint entirely from memory and imagination, make poems and spin dreams. That also needs to be done.

A great Parisian painter whom a young artist asked for advice once said: 'Young man, if you want to be a painter, don't forget that above all it's necessary to eat well. Second, digestion is important; make sure your bowels move regularly. And third, always keep a pretty little mistress.' One would think I'd learned these rules and would scarcely ever break them. But this year, it's a curse, even in these simple matters things won't go right for me any more. I eat little and badly, often nothing but bread for whole days on end; I sometimes have stomach trouble (the most useless affliction to have, let me tell you!) and I don't have the right little mistress, but keep busy with four or five women and am just as exhausted as I am hungry. Something is wrong in the clockworks. Ever since I probed it with the needle it's been running again, but fast as the devil, and making such a damnable unfamiliar rattle as it does. How simple life is when health is good. You've never received such a long letter from me before, except perhaps at the time we were arguing about the palette. I'm going to stop; it's nearly five o'clock and the lovely light is beginning. Warm greetings from

Your
Klingsor.

Postscript:

I recalled that you liked a little painting of mine, the most Chinese one I've done, with the cottage, the red path, the Veronese-green jagged trees and the distant toy town in the background. I cannot send it to you now because I don't know where you are. But it is yours – I want you to know that just in case.

Klingsor sends his friend Tu Fu a poem

(DONE IN THE DAYS HE WAS WORKING ON HIS
SELF-PORTRAIT)

Drunk, I sit at night in the wind-whipped woods.
Autumn has gnawed at the singing branches;
Murmuring, the tavern keeper runs to the cellar
To fill my empty bottle of wine.

Tomorrow, tomorrow pale death will hack
My red flesh with his ringing scythe.
I have long known that the fierce foe
Lies lurking, lies in wait for me.

To mock him I sing half the night through,
Babble drunken song to the weary woods;
To laugh at his menace I sing,
To scoff at his warnings I drink.

Wandering long, I have done and suffered much,
Now at evening I sit, drink, and wait
Fearfully till the flashing scythe
Parts my head from my leaping heart.

The Self-portrait

In the first days of September, after many weeks of an unusually dry spell of torrid sun, there were a few days of rain. During this time Klingsor, in the high-windowed salon of his palazzo in Castagnetta, painted his self-portrait, which now hangs in Frankfurt.

This frightening, yet so magically beautiful painting, the last of his works to be entirely finished, came at the end of that summer's labours, at the end of an incredibly fervid, tempestuous period of work, and was its crowning glory. It has caused much comment that everyone who knew Klingsor recognizes him immediately and infallibly in this picture, although no portrait was ever so remote from a naturalistic likeness.

Like all of Klingsor's later works, this self-portrait can also be regarded from a wide variety of viewpoints. To some, especially those who did not know the painter personally, the picture is above all a symphony of colours, a marvellously harmonized tapestry that in spite of its brilliant hues gives a sense of tranquillity and nobility. Others see in it a last bold and even desperate attempt to win freedom from the object. The face is painted like a landscape, the hair reminiscent of leaves and the bark of trees, the eye sockets like clefts in rock. They say that this painting is reminiscent of nature only as some mountain ridges remind us of human faces, some branches of trees remind us of hands and legs – all very remotely, merely symbolically. But there are many who, on the contrary, see only the object in this work, only Klingsor's face, analysed and interpreted by the artist himself with unsparing psychological insight – an enormous confession, a ruthless, crying, moving, terrifying *peccavi*. Still others, and these included some of his bitterest opponents, see in this portrait merely a product of and the evidence for Klingsor's alleged madness. They compare the head in the picture with the naturalistic original, with photographs, and detect in the distortions and exaggerations of the shapes negroid, degenerate, atavistic, animal features. Some of these critics dwell on the idolatrous and fantastic aspects of this picture; they see in it a kind of monomaniac self-adoration, a blasphemous self-glorification, a kind of religious megalomania. All such interpretations are possible, and many more.

During the days he was painting this portrait Klingsor did not go out, except to drink wine at night. He ate only bread and fruit that the housekeeper brought him, went about unshaven, and with his tanned brow and deep-sunken eyes truly looked alarming. He painted seated and from memory; only now and then, and almost always during pauses in the work, would he go to the large, old-fashioned mirror on the north wall, its frame painted with climbing roses. Standing before the mirror he would stretch his head forward, open his eyes wide, and make faces.

He saw many, many faces behind the Klingsor face in the big mirror, between those silly twining roses, and he painted many faces into his picture: sweet and wondering children's faces, young manhood's brow and temples, full of dreams and ardour, scoffing drinker's eyes, lips of a thirsting, persecuted, suffering, seeking libertine of an *enfant perdu*. But he built up the head majestically and brutally, made it into a jungle idol, a jealous, self-infatuated Jehovah, a totem to whom first-born babes and virgins might be sacrificed. Those were a few of his faces. Another was the face of the doomed and decaying man who accepted his fate: moss grew on his skull, the old teeth stood askew, cracks ran through the white skin, and scales and mould grew in the cracks. These are the features that some friends particularly love the painting for. They say: this is man, ecce homo, here is the weary, greedy, wild, childlike, and sophisticated man of our late age, dying European man who wants to die, overstrung by every longing, sick from every vice, enraptured by knowledge of his doom, ready for any kind of progress, ripe for any kind of retrogression, submitting to fate and pain like the drug addict to his poison, lonely, hollowed-out, age-old, at once Faust and Karamazov, beast and sage, wholly exposed, wholly without ambition, wholly naked, filled with childish dread of death and filled with weary readiness to die.

And still more remotely, still deeper behind all these faces, slept remoter, deeper, older faces, prehuman, animal, vegetable, stony, as if the last man on earth in the moment before death were recalling once again with the speed of dream all the forms of past ages when the universe was young.

In those madly intense days Klingsor lived like an ecstatic. Nights, he loaded himself with wine, and then would stand, candle in his hand, before the old mirror, study his face in the glass, the woefully grinning face of the habitual drinker. One night he had a girl with him on the couch in the studio, and while he pressed her naked body against his he stared with reddened eyes over her shoulder into the mirror, saw beside her unbound hair his distorted face, full of lust and full of abhorrence of lust. He told her to come back next day, but she had become frightened and did not return.

He slept little at night. Often he awoke from dreadful dreams, his face sweaty, in savage temper and weary of life. But soon he would jump up and stare into the mirror, reading the desolate landscape of those distraught features, examining it gloomily, hatefully, or smilingly, as if gloating over its devastation. He had a dream in which he saw himself being tortured; nails were driven into his eyes, his nostrils pulled apart with hooks. And on the cover of a book that lay to hand he made a charcoal drawing of this tortured face, with the nails in the eyes. We found the strange drawing after his death. Another time, attacked by a bout of facial neuralgia, he hung writhing over the back of a chair, laughing and screaming with pain, but still holding his distorted face to the glass of the mirror, studying the twitches, ridiculing the tears.

And it was not only his face, or his thousand faces, that he painted into this picture, not only his eyes and lips, the pained ravine of his mouth, the cleft cliffs of his forehead, his rootlike hands, his twitching fingers, the mockery of reason, the death in his eyes. In his idiosyncratic, overcrowded, concise, and jagged brush script he painted his life along with it, his love, his faith, his despair. He painted a band of naked women along with it, driven by in the raging wind like birds, slaughtered victims for the idol Klingsor, and he painted a youth with a suicide's face, also temples and woods, an old bearded god, mighty and stupid, a woman's breast split open by a dagger, butterflies with faces on their wings, and at the back of the picture, on the brink of chaos, Death, a grey ghost driving a spear small as a needle into the brain of Klingsor.

When he had painted for hours, restlessness drove him to his feet. Uneasily, unsteadily, he paced his rooms, the doors slamming behind him, pulled bottles from the cupboard, pulled books from the shelves, rugs from the tables, lay on the floor reading, leaned out of the windows, breathing deeply, rummaged for old drawings and photographs and piled floors and tables and beds and chairs in all the rooms with papers, pictures, books, letters. Everything blew about sadly when the rain-filled wind entered the windows. Among old things he found the picture of himself as a child, a photograph taken at the age of four; he was dressed in a white summer suit and under his light blond, almost white hair a sweetly defiant boy's face looked out. He found the pictures of his parents and photographs of old sweethearts of his youth. Everything occupied, excited, tensed, and tormented him, pulled him back and forth. He snatched up everything, threw the things away again, until his arm twitched once more and he bent over his wooden panel and went on painting. Deeper and deeper he drew the furrows through the clefts of his portrait, broadened the temple of his life, more and more forcefully addressed the eternity of all existences, louder and louder bemoaned his transitoriness, gave sweeter touches to his smiling likeness, more scorn-fully mocked his condemnation to decay. Then he sprang to his feet again, a hunted stag, and tramped the prisoner's walk through his rooms. Gladness flashed through him, and the deep delight of creation, like a drenching joyous rainstorm, until pain threw him to the floor again and smashed the shards of his life and his art into his face. He prayed before his picture and spat at it. He was insane, as every creator is insane. But with the infallible prudence of a sleepwalker, in the in-sanity of creativity he did everything that furthered his work. He sensed with a deep faith that in this cruel struggle with his self-portrait more than the fate and the final accounting of an individual was involved, that he was doing something human, universal, necessary. He felt that he was once again confronting a task, a destiny, and that all the preceding anxiety and his efforts to escape and all the tumult and frenzy had been merely dread of his task and attempts to escape it. Now there was neither dread nor escape, nothing but pushing on, cut and slash, victory and defeat. He conquered and was defeated, he suffered and laughed and fought his way through, killed and died, gave birth and was born.

A French painter paid a call on him. The housekeeper led the visitor into the disorder and filth of an overcrowded room. Klingsor came out of the studio, paint on his sleeves, paint on his face, grey, unshaven. He loped with long strides across the room. The stranger brought him regards from Paris and Geneva, expressed his deep respect. Klingsor walked back and forth, seemed not to be listening. Abashed, the guest fell silent and began to take his leave. Then Klingsor went up to him, placed his paint-stained hand on his shoulder, and looked deep into his eyes. 'Thank you,' he said slowly, with effort. 'Thank you, dear friend.

I'm working, I can't talk. People always talk too much. Don't be angry, and give my friends my regards. Tell them I love them.' And he vanished again into the other room.

At the end of that scourged day he placed the finished painting in the unused empty kitchen and locked the door. He never showed it to anyone. Then he took Veronal and slept through a whole day and night. Then he washed, shaved, put on clean clothes, rode into town, and bought fruit and cigarettes to give to Gina.

Biography in Paladin Books

Aneurin Bevan (Vols 1 & 2)   **£3.95** ☐
Michael Foot   each
The classic political biography of post-war politics.

The Unknown Orwell   **£2.95** ☐
Peter Stansky and William Abrahams
Introduces Eric Blair, of Eton and the Indian Imperial Police. In analysing his background, the authors have given us a uniquely valuable key to one of our most important literary figures.

Orwell: The Transformation   **£2.95** ☐
Peter Stansky and William Abrahams
This covers the period of four crucial years, in which Eric Blair, minor novelist with little or no interest in politics, emerged as George Orwell, an important writer with a view, a mission and a message.

Oscar Wilde   **£2.95** ☐
Philippe Jullian
Still the best biography of Oscar Wilde, This book presents his astonishing life, work, wit and trials.

Welsh Dylan   **£1.95** ☐
John Ackerman
This penetrating biography throws new light on Dylan Thomas's identity as a Welshman, showing the close relationship between his work and his Welsh background.

Virginia Woolf (Vols 1 & 2)   **£1.95** ☐
Quentin Bell   each
Acclaimed as one of the outstanding literary biographies of the century, these books trace the troubled development of Virginia Woolf as a writer and as a woman.

Solzhenitsyn   **£9.95** ☐
Michael Scammell
'A comprehensive picture of the man . . . This superb biography will certainly be the standard account of the most remarkable literary life story of our time.' **Times Literary Supplement**. Illustrated.

To order direct from the publisher just tick the titles you want and fill in the order form.   **PAL4082**

Biography in Paladin Books

Mussolini £3.50 ☐
Denis Mack Smith
'Will be remembered . . . for the exceptional clarity and brilliance of the writing. His portrait of Mussolini the man is the best we have.' *Times Literary Supplement*.

Karl Marx: His Life and Thought £3.95 ☐
David McLellan
A major biography by Britain's leading Marxist historian. Marx is shown in his private and family life as well as in his political contexts.

Miles Davis £3.95 ☐
Ian Carr
'For more than a quarter-century Miles Davis has personified the modern jazz artist. Mr Carr's biography is in a class by itself. He knows his music and his Miles.' *New York Times Book Review*.

Freud: The Man and the Cause £3.95 ☐
Ronald W. Clark
With great objectivity, Ronald Clark provides a new, human and revealing portrait of the physician who changed man's image of himself. He also gives a clear and balances account of the medical world of Freud's early professional years; the conception of psycho-analysis; Freud's struggle for recognition; and how his achievement can be viewed in the light of contemporary knowledge. Illustrated.

Chaplin: His Life and Art £8.95 ☐
David Robinson
In this definitive biography, the only one to be written with full access to the Chaplin archives, David Robinson provides a uniquely documented record of the working methods and extraordinary life of the mercurial genius of early cinema. Illustrated.

To order direct from the publisher just tick the titles you want and fill in the order form.   PAL4182

All these books are available at your local bookshop or newsagent, or can be ordered direct from the publisher.

To order direct from the publishers just tick the titles you want and fill in the form below.

Name _____

Address _____

Send to:
Paladin Cash Sales
PO Box 11, Falmouth, Cornwall TR10 9EN.

Please enclose remittance to the value of the cover price plus:

UK 60p for the first book, 25p for the second book plus 15p per copy for each additional book ordered to a maximum charge of £1.90.

BFPO 60p for the first book, 25p for the second book plus 15p per copy for the next 7 books, thereafter 9p per book.

Overseas including Eire £1.25 for the first book, 75p for second book and 28p for each additional book.

Paladin Books reserve the right to show new retail prices on covers, which may differ from those previously advertised in the text or elsewhere.